Other 1632 Universe Publications

1632 by Eric Flint (The whole world is based on this book.)
Free download at Baen.com/1632.html

Recommended Short-List to Jump into the Series:

Ring of Fire anthology edited by Eric Flint
1633 by Eric Flint and David Weber
1634: The Baltic War by Eric Flint and David Weber
All books available for purchase on Amazon.com, Baen.com, and (after 20+ years) used bookstores.

Also Available:

Grantville Gazette Volumes 1 – 102 magazine edited by Eric Flint, Paula Goodlett, Walt Boyes, Bjorn Hasseler
Available for purchase on 1632Magazine.com
1632 Universe novels
Available for purchase on Baen.com "Eric Flint, Ring of Fire Series"

Forthcoming:

September, 2023:
*1638: The Sovereign States (*Baen) by Eric Flint, Gorg Huff, and Paula Goodlett
Odd numbered months:
New issues of Eric Flint's 1632 & Beyond
November, 2023: Issue #2

Eric Flint's
1632 & Beyond

Issue #1, September 2023

ERIC FLINT'S 1632 & BEYOND ISSUE #1

Cover Artwork by Garrett W. Vance
Editor-in-Chief Bjorn Hasseler
Editor and Webmaster Bethanne Kim
Editor Chuck Thompson
Art Director Garrett W. Vance

1. Science Fiction-Alternate History
2. Science Fiction-Time Travel

eBook ISBN: 978-1-962398-01-5
Paperback ISBN: 978-1-962398-00-8

Distributed by Flint's Shards Inc.
339 Heyward Street, #200
Columbia, SC 29201

Printed in the United States of America

Table of Contents

ERIC FLINT'S 1632 & BEYOND #1

Introduction

Welcome to *Eric Flint's 1632 & Beyond*!

The 1632 universe (or Ring of Fire universe, if you prefer) has been a collaborative effort since Eric Flint was writing the novel *1632*. He posted questions to Baen's Bar, and people applied their expertise. 1632 was published in 2000. Eric wanted an anthology early on in the series, and *Ring of Fire* was published in 2004. Half the stories were from established authors, and the other half were open submission. This worked so well that later that year, more open submission stories were published as *Grantville Gazette 1*.

For a while, an electronic Gazette was followed by a paper copy from Baen Books. Starting with *Grantville Gazette 5*, Baen didn't have enough publishing slots to keep pace, and further books became best-of compilations with Roman numerals. Baen's *Grantville Gazette V* covered electronic issues 5-10, VI covered 11-19, etc. Serials didn't fit, and in 2013, Eric formed Ring of Fire Press to publish serials gathered into book form. In 2016, Ring of Fire Press began publishing 1632 novels containing new material.

Eric Flint passed away in July, 2022. We extend our condolences to his family. With their permission, we continue to advance the universe Eric so generously shared with us.

Some things had to be reorganized, and this included shutting down Ring of Fire Press and the *Grantville Gazette*. Flint's Shards, Inc. will carry short fiction forward with *Eric Flint's 1632 & Beyond*. Baen Books will continue publishing the mainline novels.

The Assiti Shards

On April 2, 2000, the small town of Grantville, West Virginia, was hit by a shard generated by aliens called the Assiti. The shard instantaneously transferred a sphere with a diameter of a little over six miles to Thuringia, Germany, on May 25, 1631. This was right in the middle of the Thirty Years War.

Grantville's transference started a new timeline. Twenty-three years after the first book was published, the edge of plot is in late 1637 (or even early 1638 in some areas). That world is a very different place than our history.

Back in the original timeline, the Assiti generated another shard, and this one cored through history, widening as it went. It picked up a maximum security prison in Illinois, Cherokee and soldiers on the Trail of Tears, Spanish conquistadors, Mounds people, and an even-earlier people, dropping them in the Cretaceous era. Read *Time Spike* by Eric Flint and Marilyn Kosmatka.

Another small shard struck in 2009, taking a squad of ROTC cadets from Fort Dix, New Jersey, to December, 1776, outside Trenton. They know what's coming and seek to link up with General Washington and the Continental Army. Read *The Crossing* by Kevin Ikenberry.

Next was another small sphere. Baen Books will publish *An Angel Named Peterbilt* by Eric Flint, Gorg Huff, and Paula Goodlett on February 6, 2024 (or earlier if you buy the e-ARC). It's about a couple families, a tanker truck, and the Mounds culture around 1005 AD.

Finally, some years in our future, a shard struck the ocean liner *Queen of the Sea* and took it to the Mediterranean in 321 BC as Alexander the Great's generals began to divide his empire. Read *The Alexander Inheritance* and *The Macedonian Hazard*.

Eric Flint's 1632 & Beyond will publish stories from the 1632, Time Spike, and Alexander Inheritance timelines.

Individual issues are available, but we encourage you to purchase a subscription. That will be the only way to access bonus content on the 1632Magazine.com website. This will include articles about writing, the 1632 universe, the other Assiti Shards, and the occasional story.

INTRODUCTION

The Magdeburg Messenger

This section is short stories and novelettes set in the 1632 universe. It acknowledges our predecessor publication, the *Grantville Gazette*.

Issue 1 begins with "An Exchange of Favours" by Jody Lynn Nye. This is an excerpt from an upcoming novel set in England, in the days immediately before the escape from the Tower (*1634: The Baltic War*). We thank Toni Weisskopf, publisher at Baen Books, for permission to publish this story.

Next is "On the Jerichow Road" by S. M. Stirling and Virginia DeMarce. S. M. Stirling is known for his Nantucket alternate history series, Draka series, and Emberverse series. Virginia's first 1632 story was in *Grantville Gazette* 1. She is responsible for "the grid" of all the up-time characters. "On the Jerichow Road" is about close-to-the-ground perspectives in Magdeburg Province.

"Ill-Met in the Marshes" by Garrett W. Vance continues the story of the Japanese expatriates from "All God's Children in the Burning East" (in *Ring of Fire III*). This is probably the most-requested sequel in 1632 short fiction.

"Indian Tea" by Chuck Thompson takes us back to the early days in 1631. A villager who needs help getting in the harvest approaches an up-timer.

The Assiti Shards

This section is for stories set in the *Time Spike* and *Alexander Inheritance* timelines.

This issue has the first Alexander Inheritance short story, "Into the Dark" by Iver P. Cooper. It's about finding the right person to find the right resource. Even though it's a different timeline, there are some commonalities with the 1632 universe.

The State Library Papers

The Grantville High School library is now the State Library. Paid researchers compile all manner of reports, and these are available for purchase. It's the inspiration for our non-fiction section.

These are articles either about 1632 or that supply technical background. This issue's article does both.

In "Farm Equipment That Came Through the Ring of Fire," George Grant details what he saw in the Mannington area, and it's not what you might expect. (Mannington, WV, is the real-world town Grantville is modeled on.)

Columns

In this issue we remember Eric Flint and Jose Clavell.

We review a few key points in the 1632 timeline as well as a few characters and concepts. If you're new to the 1632 universe, you might want to read this, or you might want to skip the spoilers and go straight to the next item.

We have many people to thank.

Finally, we list the 1632 and Assiti Shards books coming up from Baen Books.

* * *

The Magdeburg Messenger

An Exchange of Favours

Jody Lynn Nye

England
April, 1634

Margaret de Beauchamp, eldest surviving child of Baronet Sir Timothy de Beauchamp of Churnet and Trent, waited patiently on a bench in the outer court of the Palace of Whitehall, nervous to see the king or Lord Cork. Such exalted personages were so far above her station that she trembled inwardly, but recalled the import of why she had come all the way to London from Staffordshire. She kept her back straight, not that her stiff, tight-waisted bodice would allow her to slouch, and arranged her voluminous woolen skirts so they didn't weigh too heavily on her knees. She hoped her long brown hair hadn't escaped from its array of sausage-like tresses.

Courtiers and court ladies in their gorgeous silken clothes and shining coiled hair passed in and out of the enormous double doors, careful not to cause the portals to make a sound as pleas were being heard within.

No question but it was going to be a long wait. She had been lucky to secure a spot on one of the plain wooden benches against the deep brown linenfold wall. Others milled around.

Lovely clothing the men and ladies of the court wore. The men's clothes were as bright and showy as peacocks, in blossoming tunics with slashed sleeves, knee-length trousers, and hose made of Ottoman silk and Venetian velvets. The ladies looked no less brilliant, with touches of embroidery and lace enlivening their oversized, starched white collars, perhaps in defiance of the enemy French making an edict against lace trim on one's clothing only this year. Hair was scraped severely back from the face except for a few curls allowed to dance impishly upon the forehead and fastened at the back with many pins. The side locks were curled in sausages close to the cheeks, not unlike the cylindrical hair-stalls of three centuries past. She envied those whose station and wealth allowed them to wear silk and eastern fabrics, then chided herself.

Why should she be ashamed of who she was? *Her* station was nothing of which she ought to be ashamed. The eldest daughter of a landed baronet—and a fine estate it was, too!—had as much place here as any of those with loftier titles. She had been taught to walk in the fashionable French mode by their neighbor Lady Pierce with her back straight and her hips thrust forward. Still, to be able to gleam as reflected fire like the enveloping russet gown of the chestnut-haired lady just going by would have suited her so well and lit up her plain brown hair and ruddy cheeks, making her seem more than a country girl.

She had to settle for the best and finest worsted cloth that the Staffordshire guilds could devise, dyed a deep rare blue, every panel subtly different. Would any of the passersby know the difference? Even her maid, who waited on a bench outwith the anteroom, wore goods of outstanding quality. And even the brightest of silk no doubt concealed wool petticoats to keep out the chill of the palace. Finery was only the surface. It was the spirit underneath that gave one character.

Vanity! she thought, with a shake of her head. Her confessor would chide her when she next attended services at the family chapel.

She smiled wryly at herself. No need to go to the confessor when she could hear his lectures in her own mind.

The tall woman sitting next to her on the backless bench touched the fabric of her skirt.

"Tha's a beauty," she said, in a burring accent Margaret couldn't place. "What's it made out o'?

"Wool," Margaret said, with a kind smile. She hadn't paid much attention to the others waiting for their turn beyond the doors, including her neighbors. This lady, for lady she must be, wore black velvet shot with silver thread, and her thick ruddy hair was wound into the fashionable sausage curls.

"So fine," the woman said wonderingly. "It doesn'a feel itchy at all. Wool's usually itchy, nae matter how long it's fulled or treaded. I ought to know. It's plentiful enow in our demesne, but warm as it is, it's a trial to wear without ye use thick linens beneath."

"Ours is not. My father's flocks are famous for their long-staple wool. The longer the staple, the fewer the cut ends in the cloth, and the less irritating it is to the skin." Margaret sighed. That was exactly why she was there.

"What ails ye?" the young woman said, with an almost motherly look. Margaret realized that they were close to an age, around nineteen years. At their age, though, the other could indeed have been a mother.

"Flocks," Margaret said, with a rueful expression, "are expensive to maintain. One would think that all one needs is clean, open grassland and shepherds to keep away the wolves, but there's so much more."

"Tell me all abou't," her companion said, raising her hands and letting them drop to her lap. "I've naught in the world but time." "World" seemed to have ten or twelve R's the way the redheaded woman pronounced it.

"I hope . . . I hope to see Lord Cork," Margaret said.

"And I, as well," the young woman said, forthrightly. "But forbye what else would we be doing here? We've all been waiting these many days for the wee man to grant us an audience. It seems the king himself, in all his grievin', is no' hearing petitions, leaving it all in Lord Cork's lap. How d'ye call yersel'? I am Ann de Sutherland. My father is Earl Sutherland."

Margaret rose and curtseyed. "It's my honor to meet you, Lady Ann."

Ann grinned, showing a bit of mischief behind her smooth cameo of a face. "Sit down, won't ye? Ye'll lose your place on the bench. There's no' enow spots to perch."

Margaret followed her gaze. Indeed, a couple of the languid personages standing nearby had begun to sidle toward them. She plopped herself down on the hard wood. The others stopped and pivoted on well-shod heels, pretending to be interested in something across the room from her. She smiled, too.

"Thank you for the warning. I'd not noticed the crowd has grown."

"Ye mentioned the wolves, but there's more kinds than the one that chases yer sheep. Then what's yer name, fine lass? We shall be friends."

"Margaret de Beauchamp," she said, extending a hand tentatively. Ann took it in both of her own and pressed it warmly. "My father Sir Timothy runs our flocks on our estate in Staffordshire. But you've come much farther!"

"Well, my honorable Margaret, that may be true, yet it's to the same dead end that we've come," Ann said, with a graceful upturned palm. "Me mam sent me to become one of the queen's ladies-in-waitin'. I've letters of introduction from past dames of my acquaintance who have served her majesty, but a'er th' tragedy o' Her Majesty's passing, I must sit here until Lord Cork gives me leave to depart, or brings me into service in court. I've proof enow I'm the best there is at waiting!" The girls laughed. "But what ails your sheep that you must ask the king for a favor?"

Margaret lowered her voice so their neighbor on Ann's other side couldn't hear.

"Tax," she said. "Wool attracts so much duty on every step of the way from the sheep's back to the finished cloth, it's scarcely worth the trouble to shear the poor mites. When we only take a pound and a half of good fleece from a single beast, only a few shillings are left from a finished bolt of cloth after we pay the spinners, dyers, fullers, sayers, and weavers. Every piece of good woolen is inspected to see if it fits the standard, and that's another cost. We can't raise prices far enough, or those bringing in cheaper cloth from the Low Countries and farther away will steal all our business. We make every economy possible, but Father will fall short this year in what he owes to the Crown. I am here to ask for mercy. Even a small respite would hearten Father. We'll do what we can to pay the full share in the next year."

"No' the next quarter?"

Margaret shook her head. "Impossible. We had a hard winter, lost a mort of lambs in the heavy snow. So, you see, it's a large favor I must ask. Hundreds, I'm afraid."

"I'll pray to the Good Lord for him to open his heart to you," Lady Ann said, kindly. "I've heard he is a sensible man." She studied Margaret's face and shook her head. "Let's no' dwell upon it, or we'll both be weeping. Have ye any good gossip from home?"

"Nothing much happens in Barlaston," Margaret said, with a rueful smile. "How is it in Sutherland?"

Ann chuckled. "Much the same, I fear. But so much is afoot here in London! Hae ye heard of the Americans?"

"Only a bit, and half of that is rumor," Margaret admitted. "They appeared like magic in the midst of the Germanies and stopped an army with but a few men. My brother is a ship's captain." She paused, waiting for Ann's disapproval and was grateful when it didn't come. Her mother found it to be a terrible disgrace that the gentry would even think of resorting to a *trade*. How she felt about Margaret stepping into the estate's wool trade had been the subject of many a heated argument, even though others of their class had been ennobled for becoming successful merchants. "His ship stopped to deliver cargo in the Netherlands when Grantville . . . arrived? He has not seen the Displaced Lands himself, but he heard many wild tales. Beyond that, I have heard little more than they speak a crude form of English. But how can that be?"

Ann looked pleased. "Well, I would say ye can ask them yersel', for there are some who are here as *guests* of His Majesty." The word "guests" bore a cynical emphasis. "They came on a diplomatic visit from the President of this Grantville, and since then have inhabited rooms in the Tower, never meeting the king at all. I had just come to London then, and saw a peep o' them before they were swept up and shown His Majesty's hospitality. They looked ordinary enough, though I have heard they wield wonders, the likes of which no one has ever seen, and tidings of things yet to come for centuries. They say they come from the future. Hundreds of years on!"

"Never!" Margaret said, fascinated. She crossed herself with an absent gesture. "If it's so, such a miracle must have been vouchsafed by God for a good reason."

"I'm sure it has that," Ann agreed, "though poor mortals such as we can only guess at it." She shook her head, and her curls danced.

Margaret's curiosity began to get the better of her. Such amazing creatures were only steps away. "But the Tower is under heavy guard!"

Ann smiled. "A few shillings make a good key to that lock. A few of the gentlemen here have gone to have a gawk. I must admit I'm dyin' to do it mysel', but I dare not. A queen's lady must not show unseemly curiosity. But we dinna hae to turn away and stop up our ears if someone we know and trust *happens to tell us all about it*." Her chestnut-colored eyebrows rose with clear meaning.

Margaret sat back on the bench. What a marvel! If indeed people had come from the future, the world was even more wondrous than she could conceive. Her mind spun with all the things she could ask them. What would the world become? Whom would she marry? (The very question made her blush.) What were they doing here in their past, and what did they think about it? Surely centuries in the future people would be living among the clouds like angels, not on the muddy Earth, and wearing clothes made of sunbeams that never got cold, no matter what the weather.

Or, would they? Mayhap they would still make use of the natural resources that folks now employed—like wool, perhaps?

"Tell me, how were their clothes?" she asked.

"Oh, nothin' out o' the ordinary," Ann said. Her eyes twinkled. "Yer bound to do it, aren't ye?"

Margaret blushed again. "I shouldn't."

"Why not? Who ailse will tell me what they're like?"

The big doors opened. Everyone in the anteroom fell silent. A couple of men-at-law in their long black gowns gathered up their satchels with an expectant air. A narrow-faced man in modest though good black wool breeches and a tunic emerged.

"My lords and ladies, his lordship will hear no more cases today," he said. His eyes told Margaret he hated to be the bearer of disappointment, but his set jaw showed he had no choice. "Pray return at eleven of the clock tomorrow."

"Now's your chance," Ann whispered, gathering her full silk skirts in both hands. "I must return to my auntie in our rooms. I'll hold a place for ye on the morrow. Go now!"

Margaret needed no further spur. "Tomorrow," she promised.

* * *

From the boat that had brought them along the Thames to the Tower, Margaret's maidservant cast worried eyes at the deep stone archway under which they passed. It had to be nine or ten ells thick. Margaret thought the Tower's walls must be able to withstand musket and cannon fire for weeks of bombardment, and the mighty keep that rose foursquare above them was also powerfully constructed. Those within were safe as a chick in the egg, though so many of them had no choice in the matter.

"Your destination is here, my lady." The Yeoman Warder stopped beside a low doorway with a pointed stone arch. He had a kind face, and the humor in his eyes told Margaret he had heard everything that she and Hettie had said. His voice was thick with a Lancastrian accent, not miles from where the two of them had come. "I shall inquire if the guests within wish to receive you."

His free hand, the one not holding the halberd, turned up slightly to reveal the palm. Margaret took his meaning at once and reached for her purse. The Warder glanced away as she put a coin into his hand. He ducked under the archway and mounted the narrow stone stairs beyond.

Margaret waited with stretched nerves until he returned.

"All right, then," the Warder said. He tilted his head toward the stone stairs. Margaret grasped Hettie's hand and pulled her forward.

They mounted to the first floor, where the Warder stood to one side next to a heavy wooden door bounded by iron straps.

"I'll be searching your reticules and pockets on the way out again," he said, solemn-faced. "In case you want to smuggle one of them out."

Hettie looked horrified, but Margaret stifled a giggle. The man was kind and had a sense of humor. She liked him despite his fearsome appearance.

"Well, come in already!" A tall, narrow-faced woman opened the door. She had a strangely nasal voice, albeit not unpleasant.

"Lady Mailey, this is the Honorable Miss Margaret de Beauchamp," the Warder announced in formal tones.

Lady Mailey took Margaret by the hand and pumped it warmly.

"Very nice to meet you. Thank you, Andrew."

The uniformed man touched the brim of his black hat. "My lady." He stumped down the narrow spiral staircase, leaving Margaret standing shyly on the threshold.

Lady Mailey gave her a sharp look.

"Well, don't stand there letting the flies in. Come in! You, too," she said, when Hettie held back. "Where are you from?"

"We come from Barlaston, near Stoke on Trent," Margaret said, following her hostess into a small sitting room, rendered even smaller by the large number of cases and boxes that crowded the furniture. A woman dressed in blue, who appeared just a few years older than Margaret, rose and smiled when she entered. She was of a surprising height, and her teeth were marvelously white and straight, like an angel's. Through a door to the right, a big man crouched over a table, his hands busy. She couldn't really see what he was doing, but as soon as he noticed her scrutiny, he rose and closed the door between them. Before it shut, Margaret thought she saw two or three other people in the room. "My father's estate lies to the south of town."

The young woman smiled and extended her hand to both Margaret and Hettie. She had a firm, friendly grip.

"It must have taken you days to get here!" she said.

"Only four," Margaret said, proudly. "We came by fast coach most of the way, to the eternal detriment of my spine. A barge brought us the rest of the way east along the Thames. The tolls cost more than the road journey, alas. Four pounds! But our coaches made good time. The roads were not too wet. I thought that we might come afoul a few times when we struck some deep ruts, but good folk nearby helped us out."

"I noticed that the English roads are pretty poor anywhere but the city here," the young woman said. "We've been used to better in Grantville. Oh, I'm Rita Stearns Simpson. My brother Mike is President of the New United States. I'm the ambassador from the NUS to England."

"Your Excellency!" Margaret hastily dropped into a curtsey, spreading her skirts out with both hands. Hettie followed suit, crouching deeper than her mistress.

"Oh, stop it!" Rita said with a laugh, taking Margaret by the arm again and escorting her to one of the settees. She gestured Hettie to a stool beside the small table. The servant perched herself on the seat with her back as straight as a rail. "I'm not noble at all. I'm just a girl from a small town in West Virginia. It's Melissa who's the important one here."

"*You* stop it," Lady Mailey said, with a look that shut both Rita's and Margaret's lips at once. "Don't scare the poor girl. We get few enough visitors as it is. What brings you here, Margaret?"

The visitors' expressions were so friendly that Margaret felt she could be frank.

"Curiosity, madam," she admitted. "I had heard you were from . . . from the future. I wanted . . . I expected . . . ?"

"That we'd have two heads apiece and spoke in tongues?" Lady Mailey retorted, but her eyes were full of humor.

"Perhaps that you would look different than we do," Margaret said.

"And do we?"

Margaret studied the two women. "You look . . . healthier than most. I believe that you might be of an age with my mother, Lady Mailey, but time's been kinder to you."

"Superior nutrition," Lady Mailey said at once, ignoring Rita's broad grin. "Hygiene, childhood vaccinations, and nutrition. We've been trying to educate people to improve conditions in Thuringia, where our town landed, during what more sensationalistic people have named the Ring of Fire. It's appalling the way people in this era feed and care for themselves. Even the wealthy waste their resources, as scanty as they are. I believe that we are already making a difference in the lives of ordinary people."

"In education, too," Rita added. "Melissa has been spearheading that. People are hungry to learn."

Margaret found herself delighted by the energy and intelligence of her new acquaintances. Such a difference from the plodding folk who minded the estate's sheep and produced wares from their backs.

"I had a tutor, but I wished that I could have attended university," Margaret said. Before she knew it, she had burst out with her history and that of her siblings. How, now that her brother had become a merchant, she had been groomed to take over the wool production from her father, carrying on a tradition that had been in her family for centuries.

Her two hostesses listened attentively. She realized after she paused to take a deep breath that she had been filling their ears for a solid quarter of an hour without stopping. "I apologize, truly. I've been talking about myself when I want to know all about you! Is it true that a thousand of you have arrived from the future by magic, bringing astonishing philosophical devices with you?"

Rita laughed. "That's true," she said. "We don't have much in the way of those with us here, but over in Grantville you'd see things that you've never seen before. We're trying to better the lives of the people around us. It's something that we can offer other countries. I'm here to establish friendly relations with the king of

England." Her expression turned rueful. "He doesn't seem in a big hurry to meet us."

"He is no doubt in mourning for Her Majesty," Margaret said, sadly. "I regret having to make the journey during this tragic time, but I had no choice. My father needs respite from all of the taxes due this year, or we may have to sell assets that have been in our families for centuries. Fields, manors, flocks, the wherewithal of the shearers, spinners, weavers, and dyers, all are required. If one must be sacrificed, the whole may collapse with its lack. I . . ." Margaret fell quiet. She didn't want to criticize the rapaciousness of the crown, taking all it could from those who were not in a position to argue, because their chief customer was also their liege lord. She raised her hands and noticed they were shaking. She put them down again in her lap. ". . . I hope Lord Cork will hear my appeal and be generous."

Lady Mailey patted her shoulder.

"I haven't had the pleasure of the man's acquaintance, but a few friends of ours have had some run-ins with him. Since what you do benefits the crown directly and doesn't challenge his authority, I hope he'll be better to you than he was to them."

Margaret felt oddly cheered by her kind words. She liked these Americans a great deal, and regretted that their acquaintance would be so brief. Lady Ann would like them, too.

"Thank you, madam," Margaret said. "I . . . suppose that you shall be departing as soon as you may, once you have your audience with His Majesty?"

"We're prisoners, actually," Rita said. At Margaret's horrified look, the girl waved a casual hand. "Detained at His Majesty's pleasure. It almost sounds nice when they say it like that. And you know, they have been mighty nice to us. The rooms are kind of small here in the Tower, but they're pretty comfortable. And warm. I live in the mountains—or I did—but our houses are a lot better insulated than yours. Castles are cold!"

"You will hear no argument from my quarter," Margaret said fervently. "Our manor house is as cold and creaky as a dotard, with leaks and squeaks, letting in every gust that passes."

The girl laughed with delight. "And they said Shakespeare's dead! You're a poet."

Margaret felt her cheeks burn.

"Nay. Just the mistress of shepherds, weavers, and potters, hoping the king's ear and heart are open." She glanced through the window at the diminishing sunlight. "Forgive me, but we have taken too much of your time. We had best go." She rose.

Hettie, who had listened in silence with wide eyes all that time, cleared her throat meaningfully. Margaret shot her a look of reproach.

Her hosts noticed the maidservant's expression.

"What do you need, child?" Lady Mailey asked. At Hettie's hesitation, she turned the half-stern look upon her. "Speak up! We're not going to eat your entrails."

Instead of replying to her directly, Hettie turned to her employer. "They're well-spoken enough, madam, but they could be anybody!"

Margaret felt her cheeks burn even more fiercely. Over the course of their brief acquaintance, she had come to believe wholeheartedly in the Americans, but Hettie was right: they were wonderful spinners of tales, but hadn't produced anything that would prove their claims to have come from the future. Fortunately, Rita Simpson understood.

"We haven't *vouchsafed you a miracle*, is that it?" she asked. She rummaged around in a nearby chest and came up with a tiny, rectangular black box with what looked like a shining sequin on the end. "Here, take this. Don't use it too often, because the battery will wear out, and we don't have replacements. Yet. And don't show it to anyone you don't absolutely trust, because we're not the most popular people in these parts."

She held out the device and pressed on it with her thumb.

A beam of light shot out of the sequin, like a bolt of sunlight from heaven in the dim room, and drew a perfect circle of white on the far wall. Hettie let out a little scream and covered her eyes. Margaret just stared in growing delight.

"It's an LED flashlight," Rita said. "I think I got it as a gift from our insurance agent."

"It must be worth a fortune!" Margaret exclaimed.

"Nope, it was free. He wanted our business." She dangled it from a sinuous metal tether and dropped it into Margaret's palm.

"Thank you, my lady!" Margaret said, clutching the prize in both hands.

"Tuck it away," Lady Mailey said, as shuffling and clanking erupted from beyond the door. "I think I hear the warder coming up the stairs. He always makes plenty of noise so we can greet him without embarrassing ourselves."

Margaret obeyed, putting the small square in her reticule. She couldn't wait to get back to the privacy of their rooms and experiment with the "flashlight."

"Come along, Hettie," she said, and offered a curtsey to her hosts. "Lady Mailey, Lady Rita, it has been a true pleasure to make your acquaintance. Thank you for the gift. I promise I will keep it a secret."

"Come again soon," Rita said. "We're not going anywhere. For a while."

Margaret beamed as the warder appeared on the threshold. "It would be my honor."

"The pleasure is all ours," Lady Mailey said, with a smile.

* * *

"It's all a marvel, to be sairtain," Lady Ann whispered, her blue eyes filled with delight. "To talk w' people who come from the future! Did they tell your fortune?"

She and Margaret huddled together in the anteroom on the extreme end of a wooden bench the day after the visit to the Tower. Margaret had been able to relate her experience of meeting the Americans without worry of being overheard, as long as she didn't mention the flashlight. This she had demonstrated to her friend very privately in the garderobe with Hettie guarding the door. The small device now reposed in her innermost pocket, slid around on an internal tie like her money purse so it could not be reached between plackets.

"Nothing like that. They are very kind," Margaret pitched her whisper so it could be heard by others in the waiting room who were frankly eavesdropping. They could all have done the same, and visited the Americans, if they had chosen. "They invited me to call again."

"And shall ye do it?" Lady Ann squeezed Margaret's hands. "O' course ye will! And ye shall take me w' ye. I've a passion to go and see them for mesel'."

The gentleman in apple-green silk only a step away looked as though he was going to ask to be a third in the party, but looked hastily away when Margaret glanced over at him. Lady Ann chuckled.

"Mistress de Beauchamp?" A page in gorgeous satin livery approached. As Margaret made to rise, he held up a hand. "No, mistress, no need to rise. Lord Cork regrets that he has no time to see you today."

"Shall I return on the morrow, then?"

He shook his head with a practiced little smile that wore sorrow on its corners, and lowered his voice to a murmur. "I am afraid not, mistress. He sends his deepest apologies, but His Majesty requires all taxes and tariffs to be paid this year without fail. He salutes your father's adherence to the crown, and is grateful for centuries of service, but requires the sums due. The crown's expenses must be paid. He will give you a month's grace past the coming quarter-day, but that is all."

"Oh, but if I may make a personal appeal to His Majesty?" Margaret pleaded, shocked to her core. Her father would be devastated! She had watched her brother bargaining enough times to hope that his tactics would work here. "Please, I have come such a long way. Perhaps if I may ask him myself? We would be pleased to offer bolts of fine cloth as a gift in thanks to him . . . and *anyone* else who aids us. Our woolens are renowned, as you might already know."

The official's expression didn't change, and Margaret's heart sank. The bribe wasn't good enough. "I am very sorry, mistress. The king is receiving no visitors. Lord Cork wishes you a safe journey home and looks forward to receiving the statutory funds."

* * *

AN EXCHANGE OF FAVOURS

"So, all Father's investment in me as his agent was for naught," Margaret wrung her handkerchief in her hands. It was already wet through with tears, but she had no other.

Hettie clucked over her like a hen, rubbing her shoulder. The Americans sat beside her on the settee with sympathetic looks.

"I have failed his trust in me. We will probably have to sell some of the smaller estates. Baronet Macy to the east has always been interested in the pastures in the curve of the river. It's some of our best grazing land, but he's willing to buy. Father will be beside himself with woe. He counts on every asset."

"I'm so sorry," Rita said, patting her knee. "I know that's hard news to take."

Margaret shook her head. "All that wool that we've been sending to the warehouses in Liverpool and here in London, waiting for the merchants to take abroad is not enough to make up the shortfall. I've been to see our storesmaster, Robert Bywell. The hauliers and carters have had less to do than we like, and the boatmen have been taking jobs from other companies on the side to make ends meet. The markets have been as tight as a cork in a bottle. It feels like casting what pennies we have into the bottom of a deep sea, and no mermaids bringing us pearls in exchange. We need three hundred pounds now, and as much by the end of the year. It's hopeless."

The Americans had been more than cordial to receive Margaret once again. They had welcomed Lady Ann with alacrity. Lady Mailey had immediately taken to her, as Margaret knew she would. They were two wise souls, who immediately found common ground on which to converse. Margaret wished that intelligent perspective would rub off on her and give her some wisdom to bring back to her father.

"I wish I had a fortune to give to ye." Lady Ann lifted her hands. "I've no' that much of gold in my purse that I could lend to thee, and I've my journey home to pay for. I'd give ye what I could, but accidents happen, and I may need every coin at hand." She slapped her knee. "I'll have ma father send ye the sum when I return home. He'd do it readily for a true friend of mine. Ye can pay it back over years, I promise. There'll be no hurry in th' world."

Though she was touched deeply. Margaret shook her head. "It might take you a month or more to get home, and the tariffs need to be paid sooner than that. Beside that, my father would rather die of the pox than incur more indebtedness. I mean no offense. He could countenance asking the king for mercy, or sell assets to our neighbors, but he would prefer to have the fewest possible know of our need. And with the shortfall likely to amass further in quarters to come—well, there's no end to it that I can see. But I thank you for your kind offer with all my heart."

Rita raised her eyebrows to Lady Mailey and the other women in the room, and seemed to gather some consensus. "What if we could lay our hands on the money here in London?" she asked.

"I can't ask you, either," Margaret said. "As with Lady Ann, you'll likely need all the funds at your disposal because of . . ." She stopped, realizing she almost committed a terrible error of tact.

But, dismayingly, Lady Mailey picked up at once on her thought.

"Because of our unjust incarceration?" she asked, with that acerbic tone. "Don't worry about us. On the other hand, your father might be worried about knowing that the funds came from strangers the king has clapped in the Tower."

So, selling the family assets it would have to be. Hundreds of years they had managed the gift from the Duchy of Lancaster, and it would all be lost in one generation. Margaret rose and signed to Hettie to gather their outer garments.

"Thank you all for giving thought to aiding my family," she said. "It comforts me greatly to have made such warm friends. Allow us to take our leave. I must prepare to return home, too. I must speak to our boatmen about taking us upstream to meet the northern coaches."

"Don't lose hope," Rita said, giving her a warm hug.

"Hope we have in plenty," Margaret said, as Andrew Short arrived on the doorstep to escort her and Lady Ann to the gate. "I thank you all."

* * *

"Did you hear that?" Tom said, as the door closed behind the visitors. He had to force himself to keep his voice low. "She knows boatmen. And *hauliers* has to be the same as teamsters. Harry is looking for a large boat and wagons. She could hire them for us!"

"No!" Melissa declared flatly. "We don't want her involved. This is going to be a massive and dangerous operation, and one that will be considered treason. Everyone who is helping us already risks torture or hanging. The least that Cork would do would be to confiscate her father's estates. Those are already at stake because of the tax burden. The king's a terrible money manager. It's in our history books. I don't want that poor girl thrown in prison. It won't be as comfortable as we've had it. Don't ask her!"

"You're right, Tom." Rita cut off Melissa's protest. "Have her make the connection to the right people, and Harry will do the rest." She smiled brightly. "I think that's worth three hundred pounds, don't you?"

"Harry won't like shelling out that kind of money," Tom said.

"He made plenty on his illicit art sale," Melissa said, with some asperity. "He can spare a share for a good cause."

* * *

On her last day in London before traveling home to Scotland, Lady Ann asked Margaret to dine with her. She had ordered food brought to her rooms in her sumptuous residence in which she resided, a far cry from the modest lodgings Margaret occupied. Her servants, a white-haired older couple in neat white linen and plaid woolens, fussed over both of them like children. The table was laid with monogrammed cloths, all of the finest quality. Crystal glowed in the light of a silver candelabrum heavy with an enameled coat of arms. Margaret felt honored to sit at such a table.

"At the least, we can empty a bottle of wine togaither," her friend insisted.

Late that evening, they made warm farewells, with promises of letters every month, or as often as possible. With the warmth of the wine and the company raising her spirits more than a little, Margaret, with Hettie and Percy, set out again for their rooms. Lady Ann insisted on calling a sedan chair for them, "to spare ye the mud," as the spring rains had indeed begun, and insisted on paying for it. The enclosed conveyance, borne between two horses fore and aft, with lanterns swinging like the lights on a ship, was painted with a coat of arms that she didn't recognize. Percy hopped up behind and held on.

Margaret and Hattie rode in silence, consumed by their thoughts.

"Here, now, this is no' the way to me lady's lodgings!" Percy protested suddenly. "Ye should'a turned at that corner there! Wheel around, man!"

"No, lad, we're goin' that way," the footman said. "Sit tight, lad. I know a better way."

Margaret lowered the blind. A wave of stench redolent with urine and rotten fish washed in over them. The buildings around them, ill lit by yellow flames coming from filthy lanterns, were not of even the modest quality of the street near the castle. They were heading east, well away from Whitehall.

"Hold on!" she called to the footman. "This isn't the way to our lodgings! You must have been given the wrong directions. Take us to Great George Street, sir!"

The man frowned down at her.

"Sorry for the ruse, Miss, but there's someone who has to talk with you. Won't take but a moment."

Margaret was shocked.

"Am I being kidnapped?" she demanded. "Let me tell you, sir, I have very little money, and my father is heavily indebted. I will be worth nothing to you as a hostage. Or . . ." Her resolve wavered. Worse things could happen to a couple of lone women in the alleys of London, or so she had heard. She drew the knife from her garter and held it before her. "We'll sell our honor dear, sir. That I assure you!"

The man grinned. "You have spirit, no doubt about it. Your virtue is safe, Miss. Bide a moment, and all will be revealed."

* * *

Harry Lefferts sat at a table in the rear of the inn, his long legs stretched out and crossed nonchalantly at the ankle, a sword in easy reach. The innkeeper had kept the pitchers of beer coming to the rough-hewn table of four men. The barmaid, an attractive, plump girl with thick blonde hair and pink cheeks, hovered close, sending him longing glances. She was worth a good leer, so Harry obliged her, but kept his hand on his mug. Gerd Fuhrmann did take a grab at the girl's buttocks. She danced away with a coy, "Oh, sir!" Juliet Sutherland would have scored her a seven out of ten for delivery. Felix Kasza grinned and flipped the girl a small coin, which she ostentatiously put down between a pair of splendid breasts. Harry had no doubt that action had earned her many other coins, for either a quick fondle or a more extended session in one of the rooms at the top of the dark stairs. George Sutherland had said this place was just on the low edge of respectability, but suited to their needs of the moment.

He glanced surreptitiously at his watch, which he kept hidden most of the time under his ruffled cuff. Getting two of his men to keep an eye on Lady Ann's quarters hadn't been difficult. George Sutherland also knew a couple of grooms who would lend him a carriage or another light vehicle, and Tony Leebrick looked like a trustworthy senior servant. The lady's elderly servant had confided to the guy delivering a cooked roast to the apartment that Lady Ann was leaving in the morning, so he knew Melissa's prospect wouldn't be staying late. What was taking so long?

At last, Tony's face appeared over the heads of the other patrons in the smoky room. After a quick scan, his eyes met Harry's and he pushed forward, a small group in tow. As they got closer, Harry eyed the three people. The tall, lanky boy he dismissed immediately as the necessary male escort for women traveling alone. The girl in plain clothes and a good but not fashionable green cloak was obviously the maid. He started to study the brown-haired woman in blue whose arm Tony held fast, but his eyes were caught by a pair of intelligent hazel eyes. They were sizing him up as much as he was appraising their owner. He grinned.

"Mistress de Beauchamp? I'm Harry Lefferts. Have a seat and let's talk. I think we can do each other some good."

"No, thank you. I prefer to stand. I will not be staying long." She shook Tony's hand off. "I do not wish to deal with strangers who abduct me."

"I'm not a stranger," Harry said, with his most winning smile. "I'm a friend of a friend. Rita Simpson. Have a drink, Miss de Beauchamp. The beer's not too bad."

The girl tossed her head. "Anyone can know a name. I am going. Come, Hettie. Percy!" She turned and took a couple of steps toward the innkeeper, probably to ask him to supply her with an escort.

Harry smiled. She had all the guts Melissa had told him about. "Show me your flashlight, Miss de Beauchamp." In spite of herself, she glanced back at him, her mouth agape. "How would I know about that unless I knew her?"

"But she's imprisoned in the Tower," Margaret said, lowering her voice to a whisper. "How could she tell you?"

"How did *you* get to meet her?" the elegantly-dressed man countered. "It's not sealed up like a drum. A lot of people come and go every day. The right price greases a lot of palms. Maybe I swept in like the wind and out again. Anyhow, prove *you're* the right person."

The hazel eyes narrowed with annoyance.

"I'm not the one who has a favor to ask!"

"Don't you? I hear you came to town to get help from the crown and got the bum's rush. That's what my old grampaw used to say. I'd say we have the grounds for bargaining." He beckoned with one long hand. "Come on, let's see it."

His accent did sound like the peculiar English that Rita and Lady Mailey spoke. Unnerved, Margaret felt for the bench. The big man clad in black shifted over to give her room. Hettie helped her to sit.

Feeling as if she was even less in control of the situation than she had waiting for Lord Cork, she reached into the pocket around her waist and brought out the little black square. Harry clapped a hand on top of it before it could be seen by anyone nearby and drew it to him across the tabletop. He cradled it in his palm and glanced at it as though reading a card. He smiled, and Margaret suddenly realized he was a very attractive man, very certainly used to getting his own way by force or by charm. Well, she had plenty of charming men in her family, and didn't let them get away with liberties. She extended her palm to get her treasure back, but Harry put it into his own belt pouch.

"Trade you," he said. "I have to prove to Rita I saw you. Here's mine in exchange."

Instead of a black box, he offered her a small golden cylinder the length of her forefinger with a button on one end and the same kind of glass sequin on the other. Words were printed upon it, but she didn't take the time to read them. Flashlights must come in many shapes and sizes in this marvelous, faraway United States. She didn't dare try it out in the common room of the inn or ask him all the questions knocking at her lips, but tucked it away.

"So, you're an . . ." Margaret stopped when Harry put his finger to his lips. "So, you come from there, too. But what do you want from me? If you spoke to . . . to her, you must know all. I have nothing that I can offer . . . people like you."

"You have connections," Harry leaned over the tabletop and stared deeply into her eyes. "We need help."

"What kind of connections?" Margaret asked, bewildered. "My father owns sheep and employs shepherds, weavers, and dyers."

"Men who can keep their lips zipped," Harry said, his voice very low.

"I . . ." Margaret stared at him. "I don't know what that means."

The muscular man with the scarred face at Harry's right let out a guffaw. "The *madchen* is right to tell you to speak plainly! Tell her your needs, and no more of your movie-gangster talk."

Harry seemed abashed.

"All right! Miss de Beauchamp, I need a wagon and horses, maybe two wagons. Not flashy, just sturdy. I need two river boats that can carry a lot of weight, and I need them pretty soon. I mean really soon. Like tomorrow. I'll pay good money, more than fair exchange for them. But more important is that I need people who will take the money and not talk about it before or afterwards. Do you know anyone you can trust around here?"

Margaret stared at him. "Is that all? A barge and a couple of wagons? I can easily find you a captain who will take your goods from Tilmouth. What kind of cargo will you be carrying?"

Harry hesitated. Margaret peered at him, summing up his expression with a practiced eye. He wasn't lying to her, but he was afraid to say too much. The confidence he wore like armor concealed genuine fear. That puzzled her.

"Rita sent you to me for a reason. You're trusting *me* now with these questions. Why the need for secrecy?"

"The less you know about it, the better," the tall man said, his expression serious.

"No," she said firmly. "If it's contraband, you had better let me go now. I swear I will say nothing, but I can't be involved in anything illegal. I have nothing of my own, but my father's lands could be confiscated if I am accused of abetting a crime. But I will help you to a noble goal."

"It's noble, all right," Harry assured her. "The noblest. Rita and Melissa'll be very grateful. I will, too. I really can't say anymore here. Lives are at stake. Will you help us?"

Margaret made up her mind and nodded once. She would toll over her regrets later.

"You're one of a kind with Rita and Melissa," Harry said. "And Rebecca Stearns. You don't know what kind of a compliment that is."

"I understand other people's secrets," Margaret assured him. She hesitated, knowing what shape such negotiations might take. "I may have to offer coin in advance to those I approach. And . . ."

Harry needs must have been on the sharp end of a bargain or three himself, for he smiled.

"You'll be taken care of," he promised. "You're giving me a shortcut I don't have the means to take myself. And here's an advance for your connections." He leaned forward and pushed the hammered pewter pitcher toward her. Almost like a magician's trick, a small cloth bag appeared alongside it. Margaret accepted the pitcher and urged the bag over the table until it fell into her lap. "When's the soonest you can you talk to your people?"

"Is dawn soon enough?" Margaret asked. Keeping her hand low, she guided the purse into her pocket. It felt heavy. Even if it was full of coppers, it would do as a goodly bribe. "You said the matter is urgent, but I believe that I would cause a stir if I went to the docks at this hour. They'll be up and working at the crest of the sun."

Harry sat back, clearly relieved. "Dawn's soon enough, for sure. I don't want anyone else seeing us together, so I'm sending a guy tomorrow. He'll be waiting outside your lodgings. I'll vouch for him. You make sure your connections are worth trusting. George will drive you home now. Thanks for listening, Mistress de Beauchamp."

"I am glad to have done so, sir, though I may regret my impulsiveness later." Margaret extended her hand. He clasped it.

"Soft but strong," Harry said, running a thumb over her fingertips.

Margaret felt a frisson run up her body. Such an intense, intimate touch. She wanted to pull her hand back, but at the same time, she didn't.

"Calluses on your fingers and palm. You do work back there in Staffordshire, don't you? Not snooty at all. You probably won't see me again, Mistress de Beauchamp, but I'll see you're rewarded. And don't go back to the Tower, got it?"

Margaret was glad to get her first American slang. "I . . . got it, sir. Tell them it was my pleasure to make their acquaintance. And yours."

Harry grinned at her. "Likewise."

* * *

On the Jerichow Road

S. M. Stirling & Virginia DeMarce

Exodus 16:2 ". . . and the Israelites grumbled . . ."

Magdeburg Province
October, 1636

Karl Rohrbacher paid the innkeeper and hoisted his Raanz, his rucksack, onto his back, giving thanks that it was currently autumn and he was on his way back home rather than the previous spring, when he had been on his way out of Oberweissbach with a full load of the medicaments and balms that the villagers spent the winter months distilling from Kräuter.

It was cool outside, but not raining; there wasn't much mud under his feet, and the leaves on the trees round about had a yellowed, tattered look. Woodsmoke blew on the wind, along with the infinitely familiar scents of horse and ox, hay, sheep, goats, and dirty wool on human backs.

The pack didn't used to weigh so much. Or, at least, it hadn't seemed to weigh so much. Peddling, with what amounted to a wood-framed miniature apothecary shop full of glass jars and vials on your back, was a young man's game. It had been a long time since the apprenticeship that had taken him away from the village to Arnstadt, to Rudolstadt, to the courts where the various countesses of Schwarzburg wrote their books about medicine. He was fortunate to be strong and healthy, but that did not change the truth that he was a short two years away from the half-century mark, with two sons and a son-in-law who already followed the roads.

This could possibly be his last season, judging by the way his feet felt, and his lower back.

Oberweissbach now had a distribution center for the *Olitäten*, the oils, what the up-timers called "herbal pharmaceuticals," in Saalfeld, where they packaged them and shipped them out by the railroad. The up-timers had introduced many new medicaments, but fortunately did not insist that the old ones should be discarded as useless. Reichard Hartmann had even become a partner with two of them, Ron Stone and Bill Hudson.

The distribution center was why the pack was not as light as it would have been by October when he was on the road ten years ago. Four times, this season, kegs full of refills had been waiting for him at post offices in pre-arranged towns. Some apothecaries were ordering direct now, from the catalog. Many others, though, still wanted the reassurance of a familiar face so they could be sure that the items they were buying were genuine Oberweissbach products rather than fakes, or remedies that might have been adulterated along the way.

Still, peddling was a young man's game. A seductive siren voice kept speaking to him about a job in the distribution center. Not his last season. More likely, there would be one more. Next year, perhaps, his third son could join him on this route. The year after that . . .

* * *

He looked over at the student who had been sharing the road with him since Wismar.

"Desiderius Krempe," the boy had said with a disarming smile. "Not for Erasmus; we are good Lutherans, albeit my father is something of a humanist. But because it signifies 'desired' in Latin. My father is a Latin School teacher, and I am the first boy after five daughters."

Karl wasn't sure why Desiderius had attached himself, other than that the young man wanted to hear as much about up-timers (at least, about up-timers who were not in the Navy) as Karl could tell him before he matriculated at Jena for a specialty in international law.

"Hugo Grotius," Desiderius had said in a portentous tone of voice, as if he expected Karl to have heard of the man. "He's not an up-timer, of course, but I expect that I will be dealing with their academic personnel on a daily basis at Jena. There is an up-time professor named Herr Okey Rush whose field is also in the area of politics, although by no means duplicating Professor Grotius. *Principles of Modern Public Administration*, his course is titled. Taught in English. Contrary to my father's complaints, the time I have spent talking to sailors in taverns during the past two years was not a waste. However, as I doubt that a person could understand all Germans by observing only those who are in the navy at Wismar, it appears to me to be prudent . . ."

For which reason, Desiderius had followed Karl's meandering route from one town with a sales contact to another town with a sales contact rather than doing the sensible thing and getting on a barge to go straight up the river.

Karl clapped his hat on his head and took up his stick.

"Let's go, boy; time to put Tangermünde behind us and set our feet on the Jerichow Road."

* * *

"There's a song. The up-time people who call themselves Pentecostals broadcast it on their radio show," Karl said.

Talking did make time on the road pass a little faster. Karl liked to leave most of it to Desiderius, who was more than willing, but it wasn't fair to leave it all to him. It added seasoning to the reaped fields and plowland and autumnal trees.

"When I heard it, I made no connection, because they don't sound a thing alike. Jerichow ahead of us and the Jericho from the Bible as the up-timers say it. You'll have to learn to make the sound, you know, if you want to be considered fluent in English or even in Amideutsch, because some of their words have carried over. There's nothing like that *j* in German. Nothing at all. I can't really teach you, because I'm not sure I make it properly myself. It's terrible what the up-timers do to a poor, innocent, consonant named *yot*."

Karl sang:

On the Jericho Road there's room for just two.

He was correct in his assessment. "Jericho" came out as "Cherico."

He tried again. The result was "Sherico."

He shook his head. "It didn't make any sense to me, really— the idea that there were only two people at Jericho. There were many, many, Israelites at the siege of Jericho. The radio program played a song about that, too. What's more, Jesus was not there, for he hadn't been born yet, and I am sure that the up-timers know that. The pastor who spoke over the radio appeared to be quite learned. But, what with being a peddler and all, I liked these lines."

On the Jericho Road, your heart He will bless.

"Except, as I said, Jesus was not on the road to Jericho. He went to Emmaus, but there were two disciples that time. He went to Galilee. He went to Nazareth. He went to Jerusalem and . . ."

"Bartimaeus," Desiderius said. "Not the siege of Jericho in the Old Testament. Gospel of Mark. The healing of the blind man. Jesus was going to Jericho, according to Luke. Or, maybe, leaving Jericho, according to Mark. It depends on which of the Gospels you read. Matthew wrote that there were two blind men."

"Oh." Karl blinked. "Yes, there was a mention of that man. Bartimaeus. Second verse of the song, if I recall correctly. Maybe the third verse, depending on how many repeats of the refrain you count."

"Technically," Desiderius said, "it should be 'bar Timaeus.' The blind man was the son of someone named Timaeus. Who, properly speaking, should have been a Greek . . . a Gentile . . . not a Jew at all. You can tell from the name."

He thought a moment. "Nor, even in that case, was it only two people. Jesus' disciples were there, certainly, for they told Bartimaeus to be silent and stop calling out. And what is a Pentecostal?"

Karl rearranged his pack on his shoulders and concentrated on setting one foot in front of the other.

"Jerichow has nothing to do with the Biblical Jericho, you know . . . 'Yerikov' rather than 'Cherico.' "

"Ja," Karl agreed. "Like so many of the up-timers want to call the university where you're headed 'Chenna' when Jena is 'Yayna.' It's very odd of them. You have to watch out for those things if you visit Grantville."

"Jerichow is an old Slavic name." Desiderius continued in his pedantry undeterred.

The lad was born *to be a scholar*, Karl thought, keeping his staff ready to prod at a pig lying by the roadside. You could never tell with pigs. Their temperaments were almost as variable as people's.

"There were many Slavic settlements here on the east side of the Elbe River. Those who study languages believe that it basically means a village by the side of a river, one important enough that a local warlord had built a fortification. Probably a pagan warlord who was trying to keep out German missionaries. Have you been through since the Swedish and Imperial armies destroyed so much of the old monastery church the year before the Ring of Fire happened? Has there been much rebuilding? Have the Brandenburg officials been interfering because part of the monastery was reserved for the Elector back when the Reformation was introduced, even though Gustavus Adolphus placed it in the new Magdeburg Province?"

Desiderius jabbered and chattered. In a way, it was like listening to the roadside birds—though not as entertaining as the high wedges of geese and storks, heading south now.

Karl, with determination, kept walking. After Jerichow, it would be only thirty miles to Magdeburg. Then the train that would take him home, or at least close to home. The train on which he could rest his aching feet. He would get off at Saalfeld, check in at the distribution center, return his few items of unsold inventory, and then walk only eleven more miles to Oberweissbach.

Looked at from the proper perspective, he was almost home already.

"Nothing the armies did to Jerichow was half as bad as the great fire in Tangermünde," he said. "That was the year before the war started. Almost the entire town burned to the ground." He grunted. "Well, maybe two-thirds of the town burned down. The up-timers have a poem about that, too. Not about Tangermünde or about the arson that happened there. Just that, 'the female of the species is more deadly than the male,' " he said in careful imitation of the up-timer who had recited it one evening. "Margarete Minde was pretty furious that the court denied her inheritance rights. It didn't get the town hall, but did destroy St. Stephen's Church. The organ there now is brand new—well, only a dozen or so years old. Worth listening to, if you come back this way."

"Witchcraft?" the boy said curiously.

Karl shook his head. "*Nein.* Not everything bad happens because of witchcraft. Grete Minde was an angry daughter from the imprudent second marriage of a town patrician. She married a good-for-nothing and had a greedy uncle who was cronies with the entire city council and everyone on the banc of judges. Nobody thought she needed witchcraft to get her revenge; just flint and tinder on a windy night. But that's neither here nor there. For Jerichow, it will depend on how fast they can get enough bricks, of course."

"Bricks?"

"To rebuild and repair the damage. In Tangermünde, most of the rebuilt houses are wattle and daub. The up-timers make bricks faster than we used to, but a lot more places want bricks in a hurry, so it doesn't help much if you're a small city of a couple thousand people, and you need a lot of bricks. So far, there are not enough bricks. At least, not enough at a reasonable price. It's a nice little city with a charter, but it wasn't ever rich. A few shoemakers, a few carpenters and cabinetmakers, some weavers, enough bakers to supply the population with bread, mills to grind the flour for the bakers. One of the up-timers at the Exchange—you'll need to visit that when you go to Grantville—said that almost all these small cities 'survive by taking in one another's laundry.' A couple of brewers, but most of the women brew at home. No 'industry.' No mining. No big merchants. Nothing much to export. I don't know that there's much hope for them."

"Could they make their own bricks?" Desiderius asked.

"Maybe."

"If they could, they could rebuild. And have something to export that other people will pay for."

"It's like the song. Bricks are a heavy load. Too heavy to export by land, even if the roads were better. There's a trade route that runs to Berlin by way of Genthin. Otherwise, the road goes to Magdeburg and from there to Leipzig by way of Gommern and Leitzkau and Zerbst. Magdeburg's sucking all the riches of the province into the city. Jerichow isn't close enough to be part of the way Magdeburg's growing, not the way that Burg is. Did Burg get included in the hinterland assigned to the imperial city? I'm not sure how large it is. My point is—what does Otto Gericke care about Jerichow? What does the Magdeburg city council care about Jerichow? It's out in the province rather than tied to the city. The governor of Magdeburg Province doesn't seem to do a lot—not the way the state government does in Thuringia-Franconia. Matthias Strigel is supported by the Committees of Correspondence, but even the newspapers hardly ever mention him. He's sort of overshadowed—a whole lot overshadowed—both by having the emperor in Magdeburg and by the city itself, given that Otto Gericke is both the mayor and the city's delegate to the House of Lords."

"If there was a canal to the Elbe, though . . ." Desiderius mused.

There was a hamlet off to their left, under the slope of a hill, with woodsmoke misting from its chimneys. A man was walking in a plowed, harrowed field between there and the road, with a bag of seed over one shoulder. A dog that probably belonged to the sower ran barking after them until Karl shied a clod of earth at it, whereupon it ran back towards the field, then swerved after a rabbit.

The boy grew enthusiastic: "It could run along that old dry arm of the Elbe that the river left behind when it shifted course. The province must be collecting taxes. What are they using them for? Jerichow's not that far from where the Elbe flows now. Once a person got bricks to the Elbe, they could go almost anywhere by water. Is there any reason, now that it's in Magdeburg Province, that Jerichow has to limit itself to just the town? If the city council could ally somehow with the region around it . . . Has the province changed the laws to allow for regional consortiums or cooperatives?"

Karl raised an eyebrow. "How should I know?"

"Law student, here," Desiderius said in his own defense. "Future law student, at least. You said there are shoemakers. Do they use leather from animals that peasants in the region raise? They must. Is there enough leather available to make one of the new shoe factories practical? Or could there be, if there was a market for it?"

Karl raised the other eyebrow.

"I spent a lot of time studying the navy in Wismar," Desiderius said a little defensively. "The navy buys a lot of stuff. It has to come from somewhere. And get to Wismar somehow. I suppose . . ."

He looked at Karl speculatively. "How many of the up-timers do you actually know? Ones who know about investments and such."

"Not many." Karl shifted his backpack. "There's Reichard Hartmann from my village, though. He is acquainted with . . .quite a few up-timers. But what business of ours are the problems of Jerichow over here in Magdeburg Province? Except for the apothecary we're about to visit, everyone in the town is a complete stranger to me."

"I've never even met him. But it doesn't seem to me like a good idea to let what seems to have been a perfectly adequate, useful, little city just molder because a couple of armies ran over it a few years ago."

* * *

Hans Ganzer, the apothecary in Jerichow, was more than a little dubious about the suggestions Desiderius was spouting as he bustled about shelving Karl's vials or packing them in storage chests.

"What can it hurt to ask for help?" Desiderius asked. "The town may not get it, but if the city council doesn't ask, it certainly won't get it. Even the Bible says that they should ask!"

"Jericho is in the Bible, boy; not Jerichow!"

"It's . . . Well, I guess you could call it a statement of general principle."

Karl Rohrbacher had both eyebrows as high as they would go.

They were expressive eyebrows, too. Thick. Bushy. Curly.

"Matthew 7:7-8."

The eyebrows did not come down.

" 'Ask, and it shall be given to you; seek, and you shall find; knock, and it shall be opened unto you: For every one that asks will receive; and he that seeks, finds; and to him who knocks, it shall be opened.' "

"I believe," Ganzer said, "that the passage applies to divine answers to one's prayers. Not to requests for subsidies from taxes, which probably fall more into the category of things that are Caesar's problem."

"The Caesars, the Roman emperors, built a lot of public works. Who is your local delegate to the provincial legislature? Surely, you have one by now. Have him present your needs directly to Matthias Strigel. Everyone knows that Magdeburg Province is a stronghold for the Fourth of July Party."

"The province as a whole, yes. It votes strongly FoJP. A town such as Burg, within the direct influence of the city, yes. Out here in Jerichow, not so much. I would say that we are not so quick to seize upon innovations, whereas Strigel is CoC all the way. For all practical purposes, the whole province is being governed by the Committees of Correspondence, with the hearty backing of Strigel and the Magdeburg group."

"So your delegate is a Crown Loyalist? Not the best option right now, given what went on in Berlin, but . . ."

"Our delegate . . . isn't."

"What?"

"Our delegate isn't, at all. He doesn't exist. We couldn't find anyone to run in this last election. Nobody in this town can afford to leave his shop and be running back and forth to meetings of the provincial legislature. It's not as if delegates to the legislature get paid."

Ganzer grimaced and looked around the bare little shop.

"It's a thorough nuisance having the national capital down south there, and Magdeburg as its own and separate imperial city, in addition to that. The best a man—well, a person, since the law now lets a woman run, like that Abrabanel woman did—can come up with is a standing agreement with an innkeeper or livery stable for fixed rates when it's in session. Stendal or Tangermünde would have made more sense. Picking one of them would have caused a lot of arguments, though. Havelberg keeps insisting that it has prerogatives. If you ask me, though, all those northern towns in the province are subject to too many claims from Brandenburg—if we had been given a choice and picked one of them, we could have awoken one morning and found our provincial capital in a different province—if somebody at the highest levels should decide that it would be good for Brandenburg to have more FoJP voters, even FoJP voters on the conservative end of the party rather than the CoC extremists, for example. There are few enough people north of the Havel that Strigel might decide he could spare them."

"Surely they wouldn't . . ." Karl began. "Not so soon after the Congress of Copenhagen rearranged everything."

"They carved Württemberg right out of the middle of Swabia when it suited them," Desiderius pointed out.

"But they didn't then go and put the capital of Swabia in Stuttgart, in the middle of Württemberg."

Desiderius sat up straight. "Is there a copy of the new provincial law code somewhere in this town?"

"Georg Huff would have one, I suppose. Over at the city hall. He agreed that the council could vote him in as mayor when old Werner Mangelsdorf fell over and died in mid-term. Why?"

"I need to check a provision. Let's go."

"Georg won't be there, or probably not. He's only there in the mornings on Tuesday and Thursday. The man has a business to run, after all."

"Is anybody there?"

"Not sure. The city clerk, perhaps. And why would anybody let you look at it, even if anybody is there?"

"Like I said, I need to check a provision."

Contrary to Ganzer's expectations, Georg was not only there, but let Desiderius page through his copy of the law code of Magdeburg Province. It was not, as yet, a very substantial volume.

"That's what they did. They just carved out a small portion of the new imperial city of Magdeburg and made it a—"

He cleared his throat and spoke in formal tones:

" 'Distinct territory under full ownership, exclusive dominion, and sovereign authority and jurisdiction of the province of Magdeburg.' "

Karl frowned. "Wasn't it . . . not very smart of them to set up a situation where, if in some future decade it happens that the province and city are not of the same party, the province that is the city could arrest and imprison the legislature and the governor of the province that the city was carved from? Or confiscate all of the province's files? The cadasters and tax assessments? Hold them for ransom until the provincial governor agreed to vote their way?"

Ganzer looked over Desiderius's shoulder. "Does it say exactly where in Magdeburg—in the imperial city, that is—this 'distinct territory' that is our provincial capital is located?"

"Not here. There must be information about that somewhere. Werner Mangelsdorf would have known where they met in 1634, if he hadn't dropped dead, but that was two years ago. It may be somewhere else by now."

"Was it in the newspapers?"

"Not that I ever saw. There was an article the other day about temporary quarters and permanent quarters for Governor Strigel and his staff, but nothing in the way of a map." Georg shrugged his shoulders. "I'm not even sure exactly what the borders of the expanded city of Magdeburg are. I was there, once. I'm pretty sure there's no room for the province to have offices in the Altstadt, given how much stuff the emperor has built there. Maybe in one of the new suburbs."

Ganzer sighed. "I sure hope they didn't put the offices south of the old city. There's only a tiny little tail end of Magdeburg Province south of the city. More than half of it is north of here— north of Jerichow and Tangermünde. Come to think of it, Stendal wouldn't have made a bad provincial capital at all, being a bit to our northwest. It's about in the center, as close as anyone would be likely to get."

"Wonder why they didn't put it in Stendal, then?" That was Karl Rohrbacher.

The mayor grimaced. "The capital of Magdeburg Province is probably located in the city of Greater Magdeburg because for his own reasons our exalted emperor, Gustavus Adolphus, wanted it there. Those reasons were most probably that it would make it easier for him to exert his influence over the city government and the provincial government and the national government, all without leaving his office in the new imperial palace. And the up-timers with much on their plate didn't notice the problem, if any of them ever gave us a thought at all, while Matthias Strigel figured it was all to the good for him to be down where most of the population and just about all of its industry are, the better to politick with the rest of the high-ups in the FoJP from other provinces and collude with— whomever he's colluding with. He might have become the prime minister last summer, you know, if the Fourth of July people hadn't chosen the up-timer Piazza instead."

The four men meditated briefly on the unreliability of politicians. The best one could say was that their fits and starts caused fluctuations in the steady stream of one's progress toward any reasonable goal.

"Psalm 146," Ganzer said lugubriously. " 'Do not put your trust in princes, in mortal men, who cannot save. When their spirit departs, they return to the ground; on that very day their plans come to nothing.' "

"Or even worse, they stay alive and do something that means our plans come to nothing." Karl bent over his pack and checked on exactly what was left.

"I suppose they're real," Georg said. "Up-timers. Not just legends or fairy tales. It's not as if I've ever seen one for myself."

Karl turned around. "Real enough. I've seen plenty of them. A person does, down in Thuringia-Franconia."

"They're real," Desiderius agreed. "You can find quite a few in Wismar, too. I've studied them."

"As far as 'real' goes," Ganzer continued, ignoring that digression, "any one of the cities you mention would make a decent meeting place, if they had just settled on one of them instead of Magdeburg. Most of them have city halls that are large enough for the legislature to meet. Even if they don't, all of them have huge old churches that are certainly large enough to be used as meeting places for the legislature, separation of church and state or no separation of church and state."

"In the meantime," he added, "if our town of Jerichow ever needs to send a delegation to the provincial government, where will our delegates find it? Did that wonderful bit of 'exclusive property' come with proper office buildings? Or are Strigel and company still camping out in inns and rented quarters? Or, since Strigel is the leader of the FoJP, is the party paying his bills instead of the province? If they are providing his bed and board, where are the provincial government's files? The ledgers? Are they kept wherever the delegates go when the legislature meets? What building? In the city itself? Surely not in the *Altstadt*?"

"Now, the question about whether they've already built headquarters is something I can answer." Georg rooted through some piles of paper. "This came in a week or so ago, in the same mail delivery as that newspaper article you mentioned about temporary quarters and permanent quarters. The answer is that they haven't. They're just planning to."

He waved an illustrated broadside with ground plans and drawings of a building that looked rather like an enlarged version of the Tangermünde city hall at the others.

"I can pretty well promise you that the northern three-quarters of Magdeburg Province will not be made happy by the prospect of seeing their tax money drained to construct a set of fancy new buildings in our 'political capital' exclave within newly prosperous Magdeburg City, while most of the province, except right along the Elbe, isn't recovering very well."

Desiderius took the broadside. "There–it says 'west of the Altstadt, on a main route into the central city, near the main railroad line.' It doesn't give an address, though."

Ganzer nodded. "People especially won't be happy about the 'within prosperous Magdeburg City' part of it, given that the Magdeburg officials could let our money be spent on building those nice new offices in such a desirable location and then take them over for themselves. Or the FoJP could get Gericke to apply eminent domain, then buy them cheap, and have a nice party headquarters. One that we up here paid for building. What's to prevent them? Not some empty words on a piece of paper saying that a nice, big, square block in Greater Magdeburg belongs to the Province."

"The emperor?" Karl suggested tentatively.

"What does he care? If it would give him a political advantage at the moment it was happening, he'd just wink. After all, he was right here in Jerichow, himself, in person, when his army did so much damage five years ago."

Desiderius looked out through the partly opened window that allowed a little badly needed fresh air into the fug of the city hall. He saw . . .

"What's wrong with Jerichow?"

"What do you mean?"

"As a provincial capital? It's almost as close to the center of Magdeburg Province as Stendal or Tangermünde, and that's a huge old church if ever I saw one. A huge old church that they'd have to repair if the provincial legislature was meeting in it. If they didn't, the delegates would be subject to perpetual leaks dripping on the backs of their necks, which they probably wouldn't want at all. So the tax money from the rest of the province could be applied to fixing your local problem." He winked. "Not somebody else's."

"Have I ever heard a sentence more tangled up than that one?" Karl asked, parsing it like a butcher using a cleaver on a freshly slaughtered cow.

"You know what I meant. If you want to get their attention, though . . . If you want to get this town rebuilt, somehow you have to get the provincial government's attention." Desiderius grinned. "Start a petition drive to relocate the provincial capital. There must be some kind of reason . . . reasonably plausible reason, that is. Get a delegation from Jerichow together and send it down to Magdeburg to beard your governor. Even if Jerichow didn't elect a representative to the provincial legislature, the other towns up here in the northern part of the province must have. Who's the delegate from Stendal? Who are the delegates from Wittstock? Perleberg? Gardelegen? Kyritze? If they've attended legislative sessions down in Magdeburg, they must know how to find where the offices are now, because they're probably not in an empty city block where the buildings haven't been built yet. Someone in this town must know where the legislature meets."

"Really," Karl said, "the next thing you need to do is call a special election and choose your own delegate. Surely there's someone . . ."

Georg stroked a hand through his neatly trimmed reddish beard. "Barnabas Kannenberg might agree."

Ganzer nodded. "He's getting ready to turn the smithy over to his son Henning because of his bad shoulder."

"What ointments and liniments has he been using?" Karl asked with professional interest. "Perhaps I could recommend . . ."

* * *

"The only thing we've really seen of the CoCs," Barnabas Kannenberg said, "was when their units marched north to Mecklenburg during *Krystalnacht*. We mostly saw them from inside the town, where most of the people had locked themselves in their houses and were praying that the locusts would go around us rather than coming in."

"That's not really fair," his son protested. "They maintained good discipline, overall. Not much confiscation of supplies. Hardly any looting."

"True," Georg Huff said. "None of them came in to root out our anti-Semites."

"When their organizers were here that one time—before the election in 1634, the only time any of them came—they may have called us 'locals' and made it clear they didn't see any potential here, but they do keep lists. They probably noticed then that we didn't have any Semites to be anti, so to speak."

Henning Kannenberg grinned. "Or any witches, either. The peasants have plenty of superstitious practices, out in the countryside, that are designed to keep witchcraft away, but as I told one of those fellows, the customs clearly work, because there really isn't any witchcraft around."

His father frowned. "The pastor would rebuke you for such irreverence."

"It's not as if he hasn't rebuked me plenty of times before."

"What kind of practices?" Karl asked with interest.

"Well. They strew a newborn calf with salt and dill to keep curses away from it. They use a lot of dill, generally, in their barns and stalls. After they muck out a stall, they throw dill powder into it three times, backwards, against witchcraft. There's a lot of doing things backwards, such as a farmer making sure when he's bought a new ox, to back it into the stall the first time he puts it in the barn, putting the shoes on a new horse on the hoofs backwards, just long enough to lead him to his new home but cause the witches to think the animal has gone away instead of coming there. We get quite a bit of that in the smithy, we do. It's a bit of an art not to damage the hooves when a man mounts those shoes backwards. To keep birds from eating newly planted peas, the person doing the planting puts three peas in his mouth, or her mouth, and holds them there until the planting is done, then spits them out into the last hole."

Desiderius, a child of the city, blinked and said . . .

"Oh."

Karl smiled to himself as the local went on.

"The pastors let it go, by and large," Georg said. "These things are not Christian, but they do no harm."

Karl nodded. As a distiller and seller of *Olitäten*, he couldn't think of any significant damage that a person could wreak with powdered dill.

"The *Dorfschulzen* are peasants themselves; they do the same things. Most of the teachers in the village schools don't try for much more than reading and counting."

Georg Huff shook his head. "Occasionally, around and about, some woman kills her husband or brother and someone mutters about 'witchcraft,' but it almost always turns out to have been poison. There was a case in Perleberg a while back. A pact with the devil can't be good for her soul, but it doesn't seem to do anybody else much harm unless it's backed up."

He looked meaningfully at Karl's portable array of apothecary supplies.

Barnabas moved the shoulder that Karl was poulticing. "Ah, that heat feels good. There were some witches in Wittstock, I believe, with an investigation. That was back in my grandfather's day. But that's neither here nor there. We were talking about the CoCs. I've never heard that witches have an opinion about the Committees of Correspondence, so it doesn't apply."

Henning laughed. "The CoCs have an opinion about witches. That they don't exist."

He stood up and refilled his mug. "More broth?"

Nobody else wanted more broth.

He leaned against the doorjamb. "I've seen Matthias Strigel. Not to talk to, of course, but I've seen him. I was down in Magdeburg the day when Princess Kristina and the young Dane flew in. They rode from the airport into the city with Strigel on one side and the mayor of Hamburg—Gericke's equivalent there—on the other. He's a big man. Those of us standing along the road could scarcely get a glimpse of the princess."

Desiderius gave Henning a considering look. If the blacksmith thought a man was big, then the man must be quite large indeed. "Know anything about him beyond that?"

"He's a southerner, of course. From somewhere down around Barby, I think I heard. Decent education, but not your Latin school or university. Apprenticeship, with paid schooling in practical business matters and modern languages. Not sure exactly what his trade was, but he traveled around quite a bit—someone mentioned that he'd been as far as Prague, back in the early days of the war. He does have military experience. Augsburg, Nürnberg. The Netherlands for a while, perhaps. Danzig, I heard, even Königsberg. The work he did might have had something to do with the machines that process metal wire, or the mills that power them."

"Henning doesn't advertise it," Ganzer said, "but he's the closest you're going to find to a permanent local CoC contact. Not that he was one of those who marched out to Mecklenburg."

"A man has to get along with his neighbors, as long as they're mostly minding their own business."

Rohrbacher decided to get the conversation back where it was supposed to be.

"If Jerichow elects a delegate and sends him to Magdeburg, could you tell him where to find the provincial government?"

"Not right now. It's moved around quite a bit. Rental quarters. Every time a person goes to Magdeburg, they've built something new, and things have rearranged themselves. But if you do call a special election and my father does get elected as delegate, I could probably figure out someone he could find once he got to Magdeburg who might know how things stand at the moment. If he's an official delegate, somebody would pretty much have to agree to talk to him."

"Somebody?"

"Some clerk, most likely. The important politicians tend to be out of the office when unimportant people show up." He sighed. "Anyone from Jerichow is pretty much going to be unimportant by definition. People are pretty thin on the ground, up here in the north—not to mention that since they've been subjects of the margraves, electors, of Brandenburg for generations, a lot of them are a bit confused by having been moved into Magdeburg Province by the emperor a couple of years ago and still talk about themselves as Brandenburgers."

"The politicians wouldn't necessarily ignore your delegate." Desiderius picked up the illustrated broadside. "Not if he showed up with a very large petition, from the councils of all the northern towns, properly notarized signatures and such, requesting that the provincial capital be moved away from Magdeburg before the legislature wastes their money on putting up fancy new buildings there."

Karl gave the poultice on Barnabas' shoulder a final pat. "Now have your wife repeat this three times a week." He turned around. "You may stay here and compile a petition if you like, but it's October and the weather's getting chancey. I'm going to finish up my business with Ganzer here and head for Magdeburg by way of Genthin and Burg, then it's home for the winter."

Desiderius sighed. "My father will kill me if I don't get to Jena pretty soon. He wanted me to go straight up the river."

"While you're drawing up the petition," Karl said, "don't forget the bricks. Or the canal."

"What?"

"A couple of other ideas that our young friend here had as we were walking along the Jerichow Road." He explained.

"Don't worry." Henning and Georg grinned at one another. "You two go on about your business. We can handle this."

On the Jericho Road you will answer His call.

* * *

Ill-Met in the Marshes

Garrett W. Vance

Editor's Note: This is the sequel to "All God's Children in the Burning East" (*Ring of Fire III*) about the Japanese expatriates in southeast Asia who intend to emigrate to Europe.

Nihonmachi, Phnom Penh, Kingdom of Khmer 1635

Nishioka Momo stood in the middle of their modest little dwelling on the outskirts of Phnom Penh's *Nihonmachi* ("Japanese Town"). She stared at the empty crates their Dutch friends had provided for the upcoming move. Where to start? How does one begin packing up a life to take to some far, unknown place? She had been too young to remember much about when she and her parents had been driven out of their native Japan, and she hadn't been able to bring anything when they left Ayutthaya, simply abandoning all their possessions as they fled the flames of their burning village into the night.

She and her husband Yoriaki had lived here in Cambodia for five years, ever since the cruel pretender king of Siam had driven them out of the *Nihonmachi* that once lay beside the slow, warm waters of the Chao Phraya River on the southern edge of the great Siamese capital of Ayutthaya. Phnom Penh was a different kind of place. Her husband faced dangers on the river that were unknown back in the Siamese capitol. The *Nihonmachi* they found here was pleasant enough, a thriving community, but somehow, to her and to many of her fellow refugees, it wasn't *home*, and she had feared it never would be. Now she would never know.

Their daughter Hana had been born here in Phnom Penh. Momo's parents, who had known much pain and persecution in their lives, had died here, succumbing to one of the mysterious wasting sicknesses that infested the torpid waters of the Mekong River. She gazed at their modest shrine perched on the wall, their funeral urns placed on the shelf beside a crucifix and a small statue of Mother Mary to keep them company. The porcelain figurine actually depicted Kannon-Sama, the kindly goddess of mercy, but the secret *kirishitan* of Japan used her as a substitute for the Mother of God. It had come all the way from Japan with them, and was the one thing her mother had insisted on carrying with her when they had been forced to desert their home on that terrible night.

She took a moment to bow her head in prayer for guidance. When she opened her eyes a sense of resolution filled her. *There.* She would begin with them, her beloved parents. They had never cared for this place in life; at least she could take their ashes away from it. She reverently removed the urns from the shelf, holding them against her breast as tears formed in her bright brown eyes. *Oh, if only we had never come here!* Father and Mother would still be alive, spoiling their granddaughter, filling all their lives with the gentle warmth of their love.

ILL-MET IN THE MARSHES

Her parents were given only a handful of years to spend with their granddaughter. Little Hana, which meant *flower,* was just shy of three years old when they passed. Hana had cried and cried at being separated from them during their illness, having to go stay a few doors down with their friends the Nakatas and their children so as not to catch the sickness herself. The last Hana had seen of her *O-Jiichan* and *O-Baachan* was when they waved at each other across the front garden just a few days before the end. Momo was glad that Hana was too far away to see them weeping as they bid what they knew in their hearts was their final farewell to their little flower. Mother had gone first, Father following her not long after. Momo had thought old Mori might be on the mend, as he had always been a robust fellow, but after losing his life's love he shrank back into himself, preferring to follow his beloved Sakura to the next world. Momo, unable to hold them in any longer, burst into tears . Large, salty drops fell on the ceramic urns until they looked as if they had been left out in the rain. When they had run their course, Momo wiped her face on the soft sleeve of her *yukata* and returned to the task at hand.

So now they would move again, to an even more distant land, far, far away, nearly on the other side of the world that Blom insisted was round. His homeland, Europe, more specifically a region called the Germanies. At least this time they were leaving by choice. Well, mostly. She had her doubts about it all, but as usual the men had decided everything. It was off to Europe, and away we go! At least it would be to Christian lands, friendly to their Catholic faith, or so Blom had promised them. Even so, Phnom Penh for all its faults wasn't that different from Ayutthaya, the place she had grown up in and missed to this day. Phnom Penh was still in Asia with architecture and customs that resembled those she was accustomed to in Siam, and Catholicism thrived here, even boasting two Japanese priests, Fathers Nishi and Chinzaemon! Perhaps she would miss it after all, at least a little.

According to Blom, they were headed to a magical sort of place called *Grantville*, a town said to be from far in the future and from an even farther-away land across a great western sea, a country that doesn't even exist yet. Somehow, Grantville and its people had managed to move through space and time. They had been told by their Dutch friends that it was a miracle of God, but she wasn't so sure.

She didn't tell Blom or her husband this, but the very idea filled her with dread, as it did the other wives of *Nihonmachi* who would be making the move. It sounded like the work of *kitsune*, the enigmatic fox spirits that haunted the forests of *Nippon*, mysterious tricksters that could not be trusted! The Thai, Laotian, and Cambodian wives held similar fears. Every culture had legends of strange spirits lurking on the outskirts of civilization, waiting for a chance to trouble mankind. Now they would be heading into the very heart of such an eldritch territory. It would be their new home! The thought sent a cold wave through her despite the day's heat that beat down on their thin walls. She whispered another prayer to holy Mother Mary to look after her parents in Heaven, and to protect her and her little family from whatever evils they might encounter on the journey ahead.

* * *

Nishioka Yoriaki paddled down a narrow tributary through bulrushes that grew higher than a man's head. The heavy tops leaned out over the water, nearly making his course a tunnel. He kept a sharp eye on the wall of vegetation. Crocodiles often lurked there, hidden in the shadows of openings in the reedy wall. He had been told by the locals not to fear them, that they very rarely went after humans, but there had been days where two or three of them had followed him down the narrow waterways, perhaps attracted by the aroma escaping from his load of *bento* lunches despite the sturdy banana-leaf baskets Momo wrapped them in. For reassurance he glanced at the hidden compartment built into the side of his narrow little boat where his *katana* was kept safe and dry should it ever be needed. He had been forced to use it several times, not on crocodiles, but on far more dangerous creatures—his fellow men, who quickly learned to fear the ex-samurai turned *bento* lunch merchant and his flashing sword. Over the months and years since his arrival on the scene, Yoriaki gained enough of a dangerous reputation that the local gangs of thugs left him alone—mostly . . .

ILL-MET IN THE MARSHES

The marsh was a vast maze of rivulets, confusing to anyone who might venture into them. Yoriaki had mapped them in his first weeks here in order to find the best paths from his home to his customers on the main river. After his first encounter with bandits he took precautions, never going to and fro the same way on the same day, and always checking to make sure no one was watching him on his return journey.

This would be his last trip in the little boat, more to say farewell to the customers who had supported him over their years here than out of an actual need of funds. Blom and his rich uncles were bankrolling the journey ahead with the promise that they would be shareholders in whatever businesses the once again relocated Japanese, formerly of Ayutthaya, started in Europe. Blom had some big ideas, and Yoriaki thought they were good ones.

In his own case, they would be once again banking on the talents of his beloved Momo, whose knack for cooking was unparalleled in any nation. This was according to their clientele, who came from all over the world, so Yoriaki had come to believe it must be so. He himself enjoyed his wife's cuisine with a never-ending gusto. The zeal with which her loyal aficionados gobbled up her *bentos* did much to establish the theory as fact.

Yoriaki gave a heavy sigh. It would be difficult to tell his dear regulars that today he was bringing them their last taste of his wife's talents. There would be long faces at every stop. Even so, he couldn't help but feel buoyant at the prospect of such a grand adventure ahead—Grantville! The town from the future, full of wonders and the wisdom of ages yet to be! Such was the stuff that dreams were made of, and Yoriaki relished the prospect. They would be leaving in a few days, and he could hardly wait.

* * *

Momo heard the jangle of the cowbells they had attached to the bamboo gate leading out to Yoriaki's little pier. Their house and small garden were on a stagnant tributary at the edge of *Nihonmachi*, deep in the great marshes bordering the Mekong River.

Yoriaki had cut a path through the bulrushes to the water so he could pilot his little boat out to the main river course to sell the bentos along its busy docks and anchored ships. Momo was rightfully afraid of crocodiles and snakes coming to call, so a sturdy bamboo fence had been erected along the shore. It was strange that the bells should ring now. Her husband wasn't due home for hours. There were never any visitors from the water side, and whatever had caused those bells to ring was no reptile. No, she feared something much worse, a danger of the two-legged variety. Yoriaki had warned her of bandits, and she knew he took great pains never to lead any home. Still, the bells had rung.

Trying to stay calm despite a growing sense of alarm, she went to the big, red-lacquered *tonsu* cabinet taking up most of a wall and pulled a shining *wakizashi* blade out from one of its many drawers. Yoriaki had insisted she always keep it handy, especially after the massacre that drove them from their former home on that bloody, terror-filled night. Many who had escaped found refuge here, and all of them vowed never to be complacent again, since no place was ever truly safe.

She gripped the elegant blade carefully by its hilt, careful not to touch the deadly sharpness of its curved steel. The *wakizashi* was the smaller sibling of the *katana*, ideal for a lady, according to her husband. She gave it a well-practiced swing to remind her of its weight. Yoriaki, always with a warrior's sensibilities, made sure she knew how to use it once they were married, and taught her well. This very blade had saved her life on the river shore when a lone Thai soldier accosted her as she was launching Yoriaki's *bento* boat to make her escape from the burning village. He thought he would enjoy a bit of rape before killing the pretty Japanese woman, but had instead been treated to her blade plunged deep into his gut—surprise!

Momo hurriedly crossed herself and prayed to God the Father such dire action would not be required of her on this day. Thank the Lord Jesus and Mother Mary that little Hana was not at home right now. She was off attending school at their community's church under the wise tutelage of Father Nixi, who had come all the way from Ayutthaya with his flock of refugees. Her beloved daughter would be safe there, and she whispered a fervent prayer on her behalf just to make sure. Then she looked up, scanning the translucent white ricepaper windows for any shadow of movement, her bright brown eyes now sharp and glinting with the same cold steel as her blade. If someone was here to trouble this house, she would see to it that they came to regret it!

* * *

Yoriaki was nearing the main river course when he began to feel a funny pricking of his nerves. He had learned to trust his instincts during his career as a samurai warrior, and he still did so now—he was being watched! Making sure not to telegraph his awareness to whomever was hiding in the reedy expanse's dimly lit byways, he went on alert, scanning his surroundings for any hint of movement. A bird called loudly nearby, except that Yoriaki was fairly sure it was no bird. "*Kuso*," he cursed under his breath.

He was about to reach for his hidden *katana* when two things happened.

First, another boat, quite a bit larger than his, entered the narrow tributary, completely blocking his way forward. Second, a smaller boat came out of its hiding place within the wall of vegetation behind him. This was a trap!

He realized someone must have been spying on him ever since he entered this course, or they would not have known where he would exit. This set a chill down his spine, as that meant they might have even followed him from his home!

"Hey, Samurai!" a mocking voice called out to him from the larger boat.

It came from a sallow-faced fellow who appeared to be the leader of the seven rough-looking men standing behind the boat's low gunwales. All were dressed in ragged clothes that may have once been finery, purloined from hapless victims. Each man wore a black scarf on his head and carried a long, curved *dav* sword.

Yoriaki took a moment to turn his head to see the other boat, similar to his own, edging close behind him. It bore four more of the bandits, all grinning at their own cleverness.

Yoriaki gave a polite bow of his head to the leader.

"The Black Skull Gang, I presume?" Yoriaki inquired in perfect Cambodian. He had always had a knack for languages, which served him well when dealing with his intercontinental customer base.

The leader grinned. The dark gap where his right front tooth should have been would have looked comical on a face less feral.

"That's right! You remember us!" he called back, his voice full of blustering pride.

"I do indeed. Fortunately for you, our acquaintance was brief."

The Black Skull Gang, a notorious band of river pirates, had been among the first of the local scoundrels to accost him as he began his trade up and down the river. They had first beset Yoriaki with demands of tribute, which he politely refused.

Then they sent a small band of men to attack him and force his compliance. That did not end well for them. He let one of his assailants live to run free and spread the word, as the rest lay dead, drenched in their own blood at his sandal-clad feet. Since then they had left him alone. That is, until now.

They had come for him in much larger numbers this time and seemed quite confident, despite his well-earned reputation. These were the most dangerous kind of man. They had nothing to lose and so feared nothing, which lent them a swaggering confidence Yoriaki intended to disabuse them of, if it came down to it. He would try peaceful means first, remembering that his Lord and Savior Jesus Christ always admonished men to turn the other cheek when slapped. He hated disappointing his Lord, but he had a feeling this was going to end with a lot more than a sore cheek.

Yoriaki smiled and bowed his head magnanimously at the leader and his crew, using the gesture to distract them from his changing his grip on the sturdy paddle in his hands. He had his ear cocked for any movement from behind, but that group had come to a halt, waiting to see what played out between their prey and their master.

"Well, since we meet again, perhaps I can interest you in my *bento* lunches? They are quite delicious, highly sought-after items up and down the city's shores. For old acquaintances such as yourselves, I will even sell them to you at half price, a true bargain!"

The leader grinned back, feigning appreciation.

"How kind of you to offer, Samurai! Yes, your wife's cooking is well known, perhaps even famous around here. Momo, that's her name, isn't it?"

With great effort, Yoriaki kept a nonchalant smile on his face. *They know her name! I have never told anyone in this town her name before!* A darkness spread through him then, a burning rage combined with a frigid fear. *Momo!*

Yoriaki cocked his head at the leader's words and stared deeply into his dark eyes.

"Just what is it that you want of me, Black Skull?"

"Well, the way I see it is you owe us, and quite a bit more than a discount on lunch. First there is the matter of several years of unpaid tribute to our organization, and then the rather messy situation caused by the demise of my men whom you killed when they came to collect it. The word on the river is that you and your kin will be leaving us soon for parts afar, and so we decided we had best settle accounts now."

"I see. I am a simple man, and I lead a simple life. I have no wealth to speak of, subsisting daily on the very modest earnings of my trade. I will gladly give you the few coins I carry on my person and will even throw in a free lunch for you and each of your crew, if you will kindly leave me in peace." Yoriaki spoke in a polite, conciliatory tone, but knew that it was probably in vain. These lads had blood on their minds—his. He also had an awful feeling that there were more of these thugs visiting his home at this very moment. He needed to end this, and fast, so he could hurry back to Momo's side!

"Not good enough, Samurai. We have plenty of coin, and have already eaten our fill today. No, I think what I would like from you is that nice shiny sword of yours, the one you used to chop up my poor friends! Give me the blade, and we will call it all good and part ways peacefully."

Of course, the foul creature was lying. Yoriaki decided it was time to bring the encounter to an end, preferably swiftly.

"My sword? Hmm, I seem to have misplaced it! Besides, even if I could find it, what would a slimy son of a toad like you do with a gentleman's weapon? It is far too fine a blade to be sullied by the filth of your grimy claws, you scum-dwelling, shit-eating, bottom feeder."

Yoriaki allowed himself a small smile as his words had their desired effect. The leader let out an incomprehensible scream of rage and catapulted himself over his boat's low gunwale to land in the bow of Yoriaki's flat-bottomed boat. His foe was an experienced waterman and stayed on his feet despite the bobbing caused by his landing. Yoriaki shot up from his bench with lightning swiftness, swinging his paddle through the air in a blur. It flew above the man's half-raised sword to connect with the side of his face, which caved in with a sickening crunch. For a brief moment the Black Skull leader stared at Yoriaki with a look of abject shock as most of his teeth spilled out of his mouth in a froth of bubbling blood, the entire left side of his face having been crushed into a jagged mass of flesh and bone. The momentum of the blow tipped him over sideways and with a gurgle that might have been a protest he pitched into the water with a splash.

Yoriaki was himself an able waterman and kept his balance as more of the enraged bandits poured into his sturdy little craft, which was narrow enough that they could come at him only one at a time. He deftly turned sideways and went into a crouch with a foot placed on each side of the bench, then smacked the assailant closing on him from aft in the same way he had their leader—smack, crunch, splash. The man in the bow managed to get a pretty good swing in with his *dav* which Yoriaki blocked with his paddle, but it left a deep nick in the hardwood.

That won't do! he thought grimly. He jammed the wide head of the paddle deep into his opponent's now unprotected gut. The man expelled all his air in a gasping wheeze and fell backwards into his comrade behind him, knocking them both off their feet. That pause in the fighting gave Yoriaki the chance he needed. The gang's leader seemed to have survived despite the vicious damage Yoriaki had done to him and was trying to pull himself out of the water back into the boat. Yoriaki looked at him and let out a jovial laugh.

"Hey, I just remembered where I left my sword! Silly me, I'm so forgetful these days!"

He swiftly reached down to trigger the rather clever mechanism that opened the door to his katana's hiding place. It popped open with a click as he dropped his trusty paddle, which had proved to be quite a formidable weapon in his capable hands.

"Here it is! It is a beauty, isn't it? Made in Japan!" he proclaimed as he swung the katana briskly through the muggy air to plunge it into the leader's left eye until he felt the tip bump against the back of the man's skull. "Sharp, too!"

That was the end of the Black Skull's leader. His hands went limp, and he slid silently back into the black water, never to rise again.

"Now, who's next?" Yoriaki called out cheerfully.

These men were not only thugs, but also hard-bitten enforcers. Their fighting skills were considerable, and they were rightfully feared by many. The grisly deaths of their comrades only served to enrage them further. They came at Yoriaki, snarling menacingly with their swords flashing. Even so, Yoriaki felt no fear at all, his mind and body in perfect harmony as he performed the deadly dance that came as naturally to him as breathing. His katana swung about him with cyclone swiftness, driving back the thrusts of his foes' blades with unstoppable force, clearing the way for him to slit their throats and open their bellies. Hot blood gushed from fatal wounds, filling the bottom of his boat with a thick pool and the close air of the marsh with an iron stench.

The battle was over in a few minutes. Only one Black Skull remained alive, shuddering in agony in the bow of his boat, unarmed, his blade gone along with the hand that once grasped it.

Yoriaki used the scarlet-stained tip of his katana to prod the man's chin up to face him. The man was definitely alive, but the eyes that met Yoriaki's gaze were dark and dead, the eyes of a cold-blooded serpent.

"Momo. My wife. What do you know of her?" The tip of his sword went into the man's flesh a fraction deeper, causing blood to well up beneath its pressure.

The bandit surprised Yoriaki by letting out a hoarse chuckle, despite the pain and deadly danger that faced him.

"Pretty little thing, isn't she? We've been watching her. We know where she lives. We've got men there now, paying her a little visit. I'm sure they are having a wonderful time. They said they were going to have a little fun with her first, then—"

The rest was cut off—literally—as Yoriaki drove his blade deep into the man's neck and through the bottom of his tongue with a powerful thrust. He wiped the blood off his sword on the dark brown sleeve of his simple workingman's *yukata* robes, then shoved the dead man out of his boat. A quick glance around confirmed that the Black Skull Gang had all met their demise at his wrathful hands.

Yoriaki wasted no time. He placed the katana back in its compartment and once again took up his oar. In a few moments he had his boat turned around, his movements nearly a blur as he paddled as fast as he could back to his home.

"Momo!" He cried out in a voice fraught with fear and desperation, but there was no one to hear or answer him, except the lonely cries of the marsh birds.

To be continued . . .

* * *

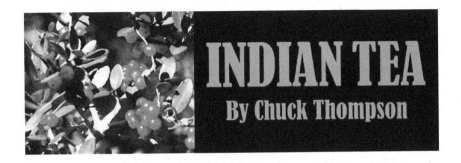

Indian Tea

Chuck Thompson

Grantville
Fall, 1631

Robert Butcher squinted at the needle and tried to thread it again. Another miss. He blew out a held breath and tossed the needle and thread onto the table. Sewing was not his thing. That was Deanna's department. But the cancer had taken her a few years ago. Robert stretched upwards and twisted his back left and right, hoping to get the stiffness out. His Brittany Spaniel, Belle, shifted her gaze between Robert and her favorite toy on his lap. A bright pink elephant. Or what was left of it anyway. It looked more like a pink amoeba now.

"Damn it, Belle. There ain't hardly enough to sew back up, and this here thread is possessed by a contrary spirit."

Belle danced a bit on her front feet and cocked her head.

"All right, all right. Let me warm up my tea, and I'll give it another go." Robert stood up, stretched his back again, and picked up his mug.

Belle suddenly looked over her shoulder toward the front of the house. After seeming to listen a moment, she ran to the front door, claws skittering on the hardwood floor. Robert walked to her and peered out the window. The late afternoon sun threw shafts of amber light between the tall pines. He couldn't see anyone, but opened the door anyway. Belle shot out and sprinted down the dirt driveway, whining with excitement as she went.

Robert sat down on a porch rocker and waited. As he expected, people eventually came into sight. He thought it would be that busybody Willie Ray from the farm committee, or whatever they called it. Instead, it was Kathryn Riddle and, by the looks of him, a young down-timer. Kathryn smiled and waved as they approached. His initial annoyance melted. A visit from a pretty girl was seldom a bad thing. Well, Kathryn, past fifty, was no longer a girl, but she was still quite pretty. He harbored no illusions she might think the same of him. At 72, he was a good fifteen years past the time anyone but his wife Deanna had thought him handsome. Deanna gave him a poke in the rib every time his eye roved. He wondered, nearly all their life together, how she always caught him. Not long before she died, she told him the secret. *Well, Bob, I just poked you every time a pretty girl was around.* He shook his head and brought his mind back to the present. Kathryn had just reached the walk leading to the door. She spoke to the young man and he stopped on the road while Kathryn continued to come toward him. Belle had a stick and was trying to entice the fellow to chase her.

"Hello, Mr. Butcher. How are you?"

"Oh. Do me a favor and call me Robert. Makes me feel a bit younger."

Kathryn smiled. "All right. I suppose I'm old enough." She sniffed and looked at his mug. "Is that tea? You have tea? I ran out months ago."

"Ah. Well, it's a bit of a secret but, if you care to come in, I'd be happy to brew you a mug."

"That would be lovely. Can I introduce you—"

Robert held up his hand to cut her off. "Let me guess. I can tell by looking at that fella that he's a farmer. I can practically smell the dirt in his veins. So, I figure this is some new ploy by Willie Ray to wrangle what he wants out of me."

Kathryn paused and bit her lip. "Well, I won't deny that Willie Ray suggested Eitel come up here. I met him at the refugee center doing some Red Cross work. He's a very nice young man with a big problem, and I think you should hear him out."

Robert waved his hand. "I don't think so, but I'll hear from you if you want. He can stay out here and keep Belle company. Come on in."

Kathryn made to come up the front steps, and Robert reached to grab her elbow to help her up. He stopped mid-motion. "Sorry. I wasn't trying to get handsy. I, uh . . . Deanna was pretty unsteady toward the end. Habit."

Kathryn smiled again. "I understand. It's perfectly all right. I remember the funeral. Three years ago, wasn't it? So many people had nice things to say." Kathryn touched Robert on the arm. Kathryn turned to Eitel and gestured that he should wait.

Robert looked that way too. "Belle. Dinner time."

Belle didn't even look back. She was lying on her back getting a good belly rub.

Kathryn put her hair behind her ear as she watched. "Well. Belle certainly doesn't seem to mind meeting Eitel."

"Hmph. Brittanys in general, and that one in particular, are poor judges of character. She'd moon over a serial killer if he threw a stick for her. Worst guard dog ever."

Kathryn laughed. "Okay. But you aren't fooling me with the gruff act."

Robert led her to the kitchen and put his mug, and another, into the microwave and turned the dial. He then opened an old coffee can and scooped some of its contents into a little ball-shaped infuser.

Kathryn sat at the kitchen table. "So how do you still have tea when the whole town is out?"

"Well. I'll tell you but I'll need your promise to keep it a secret. I don't want every biddy in Grantville running up my hill asking for tea." He paused and looked at Kathryn.

"Oh. You're serious." She cleared her throat, sat up straight, and, with a flourish, put her hand over her heart. "I swear to keep the secret of the tea—whatever it is."

The microwave dinged, and Robert pulled out the steaming mugs. He put his down on the table and put the little infuser ball into her mug and handed it to her.

"Let it seep a little longer than regular tea."

"It's not regular tea?" Kathryn leaned over the mug and drew in the fragrance. "Smells like it."

"Here's the secret. It's from the yaupon holly bush. Some call it Indian tea. Yaupon doesn't grow here naturally but my mother got some bushes from her family in the Carolinas. That woman was tight with money. Could pinch a penny so hard it'd scream. And didn't buy anything she didn't have to, including tea. It has a nice caffeine kick. I think it's the only North American plant that does. And, I have to warn you, it's uh, let's say . . . good for the digestion."

Kathryn laughed. "I'll risk it. Smells heavenly."

"Alright. Now your turn. Does this visit have something to do with the bit of farm machinery I have out back that Willie has been on me about?"

Kathryn took a sip of her tea. "Umm. This is really good. Like a nice black tea."

Robert smiled back but said nothing.

Kathryn looked up from her mug. "Okay. I don't know much about harvesting, but Willie Ray says you have a horse-drawn machine you used to take to fairs, and it can cut and lay out wheat and such and would be invaluable. We need to get in all the food we can."

Robert tapped his finger on the side of his mug a few times. "Yeah. It's called a McCormick Daisy Reaper. But it don't belong to me. It's Lester Hinshaw's, and he said you can't have it. I can't say I blame Lester for being contrary about it, seeing as y'all got him locked in the Bowers Home against his will."

"Robert. I looked into that. It's like Willie Ray told you. Lester is there under a court order after he shot at someone fishing in his pond. And when the deputies went out there, it was clear he wasn't taking care of himself."

"Pfft. A court that don't exist anymore. He didn't shoot at anyone. Just fired in the air and that was pretty mild compared to what some around here would do to poachers. And Lester's just a slob. *Slob* and *senile* are two different things, and that county judge was an idiot not to see the difference. I told Willie Ray to let Lester come live with me. I bet I can talk him into loaning out that machine."

Kathryn sighed. "That's beyond Willie Ray's power and, anyway, his children want him where he is."

"Bunch of ungrateful little . . . they never go visit him. He's miserable in there."

"Now, now. I don't think that's true. I'm sure they are doing what they think is best."

"What's this German fella got to do with it?"

"Eitel is from near Wünschendorf. He came all this way to see if we could help him get his wheat harvested. They've heard about our drive to help the farmers around here. The war has really done a number on his people. Hardly an able-bodied person to be found. Willie Ray has already told him we can't help. It's too far outside what Grantville can provide security for. And we have our hands full bringing in the wheat that's here."

"And you thought I might go out there and help?"

"I don't know what I thought. I think Willie Ray believed Eitel's story might convince you to loan your machine for use here. Right now, it seems like you're the only one with equipment not in use. I know, I know—it isn't yours, but surely Lester wouldn't mind you using it? You need to get off this hill anyway. You've been pretty much keeping to yourself back in these woods since Deanna passed. I know I could use your help at the Red Cross. We are working out of the Church of the Nazarene, at least for now. You should come join us."

"Hmm. Well, I'm afraid my answer on the reaper is the same. But I thank you for the visit."

Kathryn sighed and rose. "Okay, Robert. And thanks for the tea."

"Anytime."

Robert walked her to the porch and then went back to his den and plopped down, scratching his chin, and thinking over what she told him. "Bah. They want the machine, they can let Lester go." He got up again and went to the window to look for Belle. She should be ready for her dinner by now. To his surprise, the young man still sat on the side of the road, petting the dog. "What the hell is he waitin' on?" He went back to the kitchen and made a big noise of making Belle's dinner, sure she would come in. But she stayed with Eitel. Robert sighed and walked out on the porch. *Damn dog.* "All right, Eitel. It's getting late. You might as well come in and have supper." Robert waved him in just in case the fellow couldn't speak English.

Eitel rose and walked toward the house. Belle danced beside him, pushing against the side of his legs, nearly tripping him up. As he stepped up on the porch, he pulled off his hat and gave a short bow. He waved at where he had been sitting. "My thanks. I was just thinking of what to do. I was not, uhm—"

"You were not trying to invite yourself to dinner. It's all right. It's obvious Belle here wants you to join us. I was wondering if you spoke any English. I've picked up some German so maybe we can pass words. Come in. Bathroom's back there on the left." Robert pointed. "You know about our bathrooms?"

"Yes. I have learned it. Thank you."

As Eitel went to the bathroom, Robert waggled a kitchen spoon at Belle. "Traitor." He said it without any reproach in his voice, so Belle just did a spin and put a paw on her bowl, flipping it over. "One of your favorites, girl. Venison, green peas, and some taters."

By the time Eitel got back, he had her bowl filled and two plates set out.

After mumbling grace, Robert waved his fork at Eitel to let him know to dig in.

"All right, young fella. I'm afraid to ask, but what's your story?"

Eitel looked at Robert a moment, obviously translating to himself.

"Herr Butcher, we have much wheat in the field. It must be harvested soon. We have no men. And few able women. Maybe ten. The war has been very cruel to us. Many deaths. Many taken away. We had nearly fifty who could cut a year ago, and we hired trained reapers as well. Such men are not to be found now. We heard Grantville was helping farmers, but I have found out we are too far away."

"How many in your family, Eitel?"

Eitel looked back at Robert. Robert could see his eyes begin to well with water. He dropped his head and didn't answer.

"Shit. I'm sorry." Robert reached back to the hutch behind him and grabbed a bottle and two glasses. He poured Eitel two fingers and the same for himself. Robert pushed the glass across the table.

Eitel lifted the glass gingerly and took a sip. He grimaced but took another sip. Eitel wiped his eyes with the sleeve of his coat. Whether that was because of the shine or grief, Robert couldn't tell.

Robert lowered his voice. "You know. You could just stay here. There is a need for young men, and you'd make out a lot better working here than you would farming."

"I have been told this many times. I have good reason I must return even if I have no family of my own to go back to."

Robert leaned back in his chair and gave Eitel a sideways look. "That reason wouldn't wear a dress and a pretty face, would it?" Robert smiled.

Eitel flushed and smiled back. "It might. Her name is Gese. We would like to wed but her father will not give permission given the uncertainty. If I could get my crop in . . ."

"Ah. I think I see. And so, you been hanging out at the refugee center asking questions and finally hooked up with Willie Ray. He thought he'd send you up here with that story, and a pretty girl to boot, thinkin' that might change my mind?" Robert smiled.

Eitel looked up at him and scrunched his face a bit. "I do not know about this. They said only you might be of some help. I think perhaps Frau Riddle should not be referred to in such a way?"

Robert laughed. "Well, good for you. That speaks to your favor correcting me on such a thing." He laughed again. "I cannot explain it well, but calling a married woman pretty is not an insult to her honor among us. Well. I mean I guess it could be depending on how you said it, but I didn't say it that way. Kathryn indeed is an upstanding woman . . . and a pretty one, too." He winked.

"I still have much to learn of you up-timers."

"You'll figure it out. Help me clean up, and we can pull the cork some more. You might as well stay the night. You can finish telling me about your farm and this gal you're after. I'll call down to the center and let 'em know. Belle here would be happy to keep your feet warm if you don't mind it. She don't sleep in my room. My wife's rules."

The next morning, Robert had been awake a couple of hours before Eitel stumbled into the kitchen, rubbing his bloodshot eyes.

"Well, I see corn liquor ain't exactly what you're used to. Well. I got your remedy. Some nice salty ham and buttermilk biscuits. One thing I do not miss about up-time is that shitty watery-white stuff people called milk. Y'all got the real deal here."

Eitel groaned a bit and gingerly picked up a biscuit.

"You missed most of the morning chores. But that's fine. I got a proposal for you, but first you eat, and then I'll introduce you to Devil."

Eitel snapped his head up and his eyes widened.

Robert laughed and slapped his leg. "Naw. Not that devil. This one's my mule named Devil. He comes by that name honestly as you will see. Devil, and Gertie, my other mule, pull the reaper that I'm also going to show you. Then we can talk about my plan. I've been thinking on it most of the night. If you and Lester agree, we got a lot of work to do."

Eitel did agree to the plan, although Robert decided to withhold a few bits of information. *For Eitel's own good,* he told himself.

The next day and a half were busy. They got Robert's market wagon ready and the reaper partly disassembled and loaded onto it. There were a few overdue repairs on Devil's plow-harness, and

Robert had to get the wagon's brakes working and fix one of the shafts. Devil, feeling more cantankerous than usual, had almost broken one of them trying to back up and kick. He had missed Robert's head but had caught the shaft hard on the downstroke.

After lunch the second day they were ready and would go get Lester that evening.

"It still does not sit well with me that we leave in darkness. Honest men have no need to cover their deeds with the night," Eitel said.

Robert blew out loudly. "I explained this a thousand times. We ain't doing anything wrong. Everything we're taking is mine or Lester's. But the Emergency Committee wants that reaper, and I don't trust they won't try to stop us."

As soon as it got dark, they drove close to Bowers Assisted Living Center and Robert stopped the rig out of sight of the buildings. He handed the reins to Eitel.

"Don't let go of these or Devil will know it and take off. Don't try tying him up, neither. That mule would tear down a tree or break his neck if you do it."

"I believe it. He is the biggest mule I have ever seen in my life."

As if knowing they were talking about him, Devil bent his neck around and eyed them. Robert found this comical because the mule had to do quite a contortion to see past his blinders.

"I do not like how he looks. He is smarter than a mule should be," Eitel said.

"He likes you. He hasn't tried to bite or kick you. Does it to me and Lester all the time." Robert locked eyes with Devil and pointed two fingers at him. "Yeah, I'm talking about you, you old ornery bastard." Robert jumped down. "I'll be right back. Maybe thirty minutes. Make sure Belle don't follow me."

Robert trudged up the slope leading to the Bowers grounds. He stayed close to the bushes, though he was fairly certain no one would be looking for prowlers. "One, two, three, fourth window from the right." Robert tapped on the window four times. No response. "That old coot better not have fallen asleep." He tapped louder.

A light in the room came on.

"Lester. Damn it. No lights." Robert rose from his crouch and looked in the window. A medusa stared back at him. The medusa screamed. Robert screamed and stumbled back, tripping over some edging and landing hard. The lady, whom he now realized only resembled Medusa, retreated from the window and yelled into the hallway for someone named *Hermann* to save her.

Robert heard a noise to his right and looked over to see Lester eyeing him from a different window. "Lester, what the hell are you doing in the wrong room?"

Lester shook his head at him. "You dumbass. I'm in the right room. You're under the wrong window. You got the old banshee wound up now. If Joshua had her in his army, he wouldn't have needed any damn horns at Jericho." Lester threw a bag out and began to wiggle his way through the window. He didn't get far.

Robert stood up and hobbled over. "Dang it. We should've measured that window. I'm not sure that tire of yours is gonna get through. They must feed you pretty well."

"I'll feed you this here fist when I get out. They fix these windows so they don't open all the way. Grab my hand and pull."

Robert started pulling and Lester inched a bit further.

At that moment, a head appeared out of the medusa's window. The head shouted in heavily accented English, "Hey! Stop that. What are you doing?"

Hermann, thought Robert. Must be a night orderly. Herman, clearly smaller and more lithe than Lester, started crawling through his window. Robert bent down and felt for some rocks. He came up with a few and started flinging them. He mostly missed, but managed to put one through the glass. *Crap. We're in it now.*

"Ow! Ow! Damn you! Stop that!" Herman retreated.

Robert went back to Lester and grabbed him under the armpits and heaved with all he had. Lester popped out of the window, and they landed in a heap, Lester on top of Robert.

"Damn it, Robert. You done scraped me all up."

"Let's go, you old fart, before Hermann gets back with reinforcements."

"I can't, damn it. My pants pulled off." Lester turned back.

"Oh, hell no. We got no time to rescue pants." Robert grabbed Lester by the arm, but Lester swung at him, landing one on the shoulder.

"I ain't leaving without my pants, pisshead. You always were bossy." Lester went back to the window and got his pants free.

"Lester. Please. Put your pants on down the hill."

Lester nodded and they started trotting down the hill. About halfway, Lester fell and started rolling, cursing a blue streak as he went.

It took Robert a minute to catch up with him. "You all right?"

"Gopher hole."

Robert snorted. "Okay. If you say so. Gimme your hand."

When they reached the wagon, Eitel stared at them, mouth agape. The moonlight gave them just enough light to see each other, Robert covered in mud and Lester bleeding from his scrapes and naked from the waist down.

"Damn Lester. I think you lost more than your pants." Robert said.

Lester looked down and then back at Robert and gave him the middle finger. "Least I needn't be ashamed to be nekid. Unlike someone else we both know."

"I think both our nude modeling days are long over. I'm willing to risk capture to give you a minute to get them pants on."

The sound of shouting drifted down, and they could see three or four flashlight beams swinging back and forth across the grass and trees.

"Eitel, let's get a move on."

Eitel turned and looked back at the two men. "What has happened? I heard screaming. At least I think it was screaming. It could have been a banshee. And now there are men with lights searching for you. It is clear to me that Herr Hinshaw is not supposed to be leaving this place. What have you gotten me into?"

"It's called plausible deniability. I'll explain later."

"I will not be part of some crime," Eitel said.

"It ain't like that. But I don't have time to explain." Robert pulled himself up, gave Lester a hand, and then grabbed the reins and popped Devil on the rump. Devil gave a desultory kick in response but moved out.

They went through the night, sometimes barely able to see the road in front of them. By mid-morning, Robert felt they were far enough out of Grantville to risk a stop. He pulled the wagon off the road and behind a copse of trees. Robert and Eitel untacked Devil and Gertie and set up an electrobraid fence to keep them from wandering off. Eitel was still unhappy with the situation, but Robert and Lester had been able to somewhat convince him that Lester's confinement was unjust.

Robert woke up with a start. It was almost dusk. "Dag nab it." Lester was supposed to wake him up hours ago. He looked around and spotted Lester with his back against a tree, softly snoring, a shotgun cradled in his arms. Robert went over and gently pulled the shotgun away from him and set it aside. "Hey, dumbass. Wake up." He kicked Lester in the thigh. None too softly.

"Oi. You old bastard."

"Don't 'oi' me, numbskull. You fell asleep on watch. The Indians could have had us stuck and scalped by now."

"Oh, screw you. We're plenty safe here. Barely out of Grantville."

"Seriously, Lester. We can get away with that here, but we're headed into no man's land. We all gotta stand a watch."

Lester didn't say anything, but nodded his head.

"Well, we might as well get a move on. Looks like we'll have some moon tonight, too, so we can get some miles behind us." Robert looked around for Belle and finally spotted her curled up next to Eitel. *Traitor.*

It took longer than he would have liked, but they finally got on the road. He was a little worried about all the tall green grass that Devil and Gertie had eaten while everyone overslept. But they seemed fine, other than Devil having a bad case of gas. And his normal gas could be deadly. Because they were traveling against the wind, there wasn't any way to avoid it. Only Belle seemed unfazed.

"You would enjoy this, wouldn't you?" Robert told her.

Belle looked up at him and wagged her whole body.

Devil lifted his tail to let another one loose, and Robert leaned down and raised his elbow in front of his face in case anything besides gas came out.

The sound snapped Eitel out of his slumber. He gave Devil and Robert a quick look. "Too much green grass."

No shit, Sherlock almost came out of Robert's mouth, but he decided that would have led to long explanations, and he wasn't in the mood.

They traveled into the morning again and found an abandoned farmstead not far off the road to rest in. Although Eitel told them he had seen no mercenaries near his home in months, Robert didn't want to take any chances. Where possible, they went around any villages. He wasn't afraid of the residents, but a wagon going through at night might raise an alarm and was certain to cause talk. Talk led to trouble.

They decided to get an earlier start and, late afternoon, set off with Eitel driving. Robert was exhausted. Lester clearly was also. As they neared Eitel's village, Eitel began to chatter nonstop. He kept pointing things out and telling them stories about them. He retold the story of Gese's father not giving him permission to wed her and how that would all change if they could get the harvest in. Robert and Lester were getting worn out just listening to him, and they started a game of who could produce the most theatrical yawn. But their antics had no effect on Eitel's enthusiasm.

Finally, Lester handed him a pack of something. "That there is gum. You stick it in your mouth and chew. And you don't talk while you're doing it. Enjoy. Have the whole pack. I'm gonna have a lie back in the wagon."

Robert leaned against the seat's side rail and closed his eyes.

They both awoke to Eitel's excited voice. "There. That is the lane to our village. My own family's house is just down here. If we hurry, we can call at Gese's before dinner. We need to talk to Herr Dorsch, Gese's father, to get his help to gather everyone for the harvesting and threshing. And we may want his plow horses, too. Mighty as they are, I do not think Devil and Gertie can do everything."

Lester looked at Robert. "I wouldn't mind getting a look at this girl he's been going on about. You know all this trouble is just so he can get laid. I bet he's still a virgin—"

Robert smacked him with his hat and lowered his voice. "Eitel isn't some West Virginia redneck boy chasing skirt. And every farm boy in this world is a virgin till he gets hitched, or engaged, which is pretty much the same thing here. Mind your teasing."

Lester smiled. "Shit, Robert. That's what we were doing at his age. We never went to this much work though."

"Oh. I don't know. I think the last ones we got made us work for it."

"Both worth it, my man. I'll let you in on something. If you're looking for action, Bowers is the place. This tire I got round my middle ain't from Bowers' food. It's all the goodies those desperate widows bring me all the time." Lester winked.

"Yeah. No thanks."

"Ah. We are here, my friends," Eitel said. "The mules and the wagon can go in the barn to the right . . . and there is smoke rising from the chimney. Dear Gese has been here I think."

And still was. The door opened and a very comely blonde girl came running out with her arms wide, crying as she came. Eitel leaped down, with Belle chasing him. He rushed to Gese, nearly knocking her over. Gese grabbed his face, kissed him full, and then leaned her head on his chest, grabbed his shirt in both fists, and sobbed. Eitel turned bright red but didn't let her go.

Lester leaned over to Robert. "Damn. That's a keeper that'll miss you that much."

Robert nodded.

Belle ran around and around Gese and Eitel, barking. After a minute, she must have realized the game wasn't for her amusement, and she loped back to the wagon and looked up.

"You see you ain't his best gal, do you? Well, I happen to have a bit of jerky in my pocket and it's the cure for a broken heart . . . come on, Lester. Let's get unpacked and give these birds their moment."

They almost had the wagon and the mules settled when Eitel rushed into the barn, full of apologies. Apparently, sheer luck had

Gese there when they arrived. She had been coming every day to see to the animals and normally was already on her way back by mid-morning but had decided to clean the house that day. She made dinner for them out of two cans of Spam they brought. Robert told them it was chopped ham. *Eh*, he thought. Close enough. Gese spoke little and was content to mostly gaze at Eitel.

Lester and Robert begged off going to meet Herr Dorsch that night. They were dead tired, and tomorrow was a big day. Eitel walked Gese home.

Near Wünschendorf

Robert and Lester were fast asleep when Eitel returned just after dark. Robert decided that, since it wasn't Deanna's house, Belle could sleep with him, and she lay curled up at his feet.

Just before sunrise, the door opened, and light from a lantern spilled into the room. Eitel stood behind the lamp. "Herr Butcher? Are you awake? Time to begin, I think."

Robert sat up and slid his legs off the bed. Belle jumped down and pushed her muzzle into his calf. "Yup. We're up. C'mon, Belle, let's get you outside."

Breakfast was the dinner leftovers and gruel, warmed up over the fire. Robert thanked God they had brought some seasoning as these people had none, and gruel was a sad affair without it.

By the time the scrawny rooster in the yard was greeting the sun, they had the reaper down and assembled and were hitching up Devil and Gertie. Herr Dorsch and Gese arrived as they led the mules to the nearest field, which ran right up to the barn.

Robert walked over to Gese's father and stuck out his hand. "How ya do? I'm Robert."

Heinrich Dorsch looked at the hand a moment and then grasped it lightly.

Robert smiled and decided not to force a proper shake. With his limited German and Eitel's assistance, they introduced each other. More people arrived as they talked. There were three men older than Robert, four young women between thirteen and thirty, a smattering of children, maybe five ladies aged from forty to sixty, and one quite elderly lady. He gazed at the group. Heinrich must have caught his doubtful look. He spoke to Eitel who translated.

"Herr Dorsch says they are all hard workers. Strong. Even Grandma Schmidt will be helpful."

Robert nodded his head. "No men?"

Eitel's face dropped. "No. I am the only man in the village older than ten and younger than fifty."

Robert pursed his lips and nodded. To change the subject, he motioned everyone to gather round the reaper. He pointed out the important parts. "This here is the cutting bar. It'll cut the grain at any height and the operator can raise or lower the machine depending on the ground or the length stalk you want. These three paddles sweep the grain and stalks onto the platform on the back and the fourth paddle pushes the bundle off onto the ground. That's where you folks come in. You gather it, bind it, and stack it on the wagon that'll follow us."

"How much faster than men with scythes?" asked Eitel.

"If the fields are pretty much like this one, it would take fifteen to twenty men to keep up with what we can do."

As Eitel translated, a murmuring wave went through the group. There were more than a few disbelieving frowns. Robert just smiled. "Well, how 'bout I just show you?" He hopped onto the driver's seat, took a minute to adjust everything, flicked the reins at Devil and Gertie, and called out "Hyup." Belle ran to the front with an excited yip. Robert imagined Belle thought this entire operation's purpose was just to scare up little critters for her to chase and dispatch. They'd have to lock her up somewhere in a few hours or she'd run herself to death.

The reaper went down the field edge, cutting and sweeping bundles of grain stalks onto the ground. The whole crowd trotted along behind, at first too stunned to get to work. Smiles broke out, and Heinrich clapped his hands and shouted. Robert thought he heard him say, "I do not think we can keep up with you."

Gradually, the people got organized and were binding the sheaves and carting them away. Another wagon arrived, and more carts, and gradually they were able to keep up. Throughout the morning, the reaper clickety-clacked its way through Eitel's fields, its rake paddles adding their *fwop fwop* sound. As Robert expected, Heinrich's horses did not care for the noise of this new contraption and had to be slowly acclimated to it by watching and then following the reaper. By the end of the day, they would try one, and then the other, beside Gertie, but not Devil, to get them used to it. He couldn't pair Devil with any other animal because he exuded malice and seemed to make anyone except Gertie nervous. He and Fletcher took turns driving and teaching Eitel the machine.

Early afternoon, they took a break under a big oak. Some of the ladies had gone back for food and set out a spread. Gese went to Eitel's place to get some of Robert's provisions, and they had a hearty, although simple, lunch.

Eitel and a couple of the older children were seeing to Devil and Gertie, getting them watered and checking for rubs or any other problems.

Robert and Lester sat down on a fallen branch. "You look like a mule eating briars, Lester."

"Well, bud, I been stuck in that retirement home for years now eating ginger snaps and chocolate chips. God, it feels good to be back at this. I appreciate you getting me out of there. By the way, how long you reckon I have to stay out here living with Eitel?"

"Beats me. I'll have to send you a message when the coast clears. Hell, they might lock me up when I go back." Robert gave Lester a sideways look. "You look a bit tired. Feeling okay?"

"I'm fine, fart-face. Worry about your own old ass."

Robert raised both hands. "Just asking. Geesh . . . you can take a break, you know. I think Eitel is ready to run the reaper."

"I don't doubt it. Boy's got a way with the team. I think Devil has a crush on him. I thought that mule hated everyone but Gertie. And he barely tolerates her."

Robert laughed. "You got that right. We better keep Gese away from Devil so he's not tempted to remove the competition."

Lester brushed the crumbs off his jeans and stood. "I reckon it's my turn driving. Then Eitel can have a long spell at it. Y'all finish your lunch and catch up to me when you can. I'll get things going." Belle, refreshed from a quick nap, got up to follow him.

Lester moved the rig into position and engaged the reaper. The field they were in was narrow but long. Maybe a few hundred meters.

A half hour later, Belle's occasional yip changed to an incessant bark.

Eitel looked across the field to where the reaper stood still. "Herr Hinshaw has stopped."

Robert also looked but couldn't make out what Lester was doing. "Probably another jam."

Belle started howling, and Robert realized something was wrong. "Eitel, we better get down there."

Eitel began sprinting toward the reaper, and Robert followed as fast as he could. Eitel got there long before him and began waving frantically back.

By the time Robert arrived, Eitel had taken his shirt off and had it under Lester's head. It looked like Lester had fallen from the seat. He was bleeding from a cut above his eye and was gray as a ghost. But the cut was not near bad enough to explain the pallor. Robert got down on his knees and checked Lester for any other injuries.

"I'm all right. Gimme a minute," Lester said.

"You ain't all right. You look like death warmed over." Robert started trying to find a pulse, but couldn't seem to get it. He finally put his ear against Lester's chest. "Lester, you're heart's all over the place. I can't figure out what I'm hearing."

"I got arrhythmia, you dumbass. My heart goes wonky every once in a while. Been happening more lately."

"Shit, Lester. Why didn't you tell me? I never would've brought you out here. We gotta get you back—"

Lester cut him off. "They can't do anything. Medicine wasn't helping anymore. And they can't waste what's left. I was supposed to get a pacemaker but the Ring nixed that. Best get me someplace to rest and maybe it will fix itself."

Robert, Gese, and another villager helped get Lester into the gathering wagon and back to Eitel's house where they settled him in a bed. Lester shooed Robert and Eitel away, arguing that they couldn't do anything, and the reaper had to keep running while the weather held. Robert reluctantly agreed after Gese said she would look after Lester, which was very much to Lester's liking. "She's a sore sight better to look at than your sour mug."

Eitel waggled his finger at both of them and said, "I am not sure if I should leave you two alone. Herr Hinshaw is not to be trusted."

Robert barked a laugh. "Eitel, that's the first joke I've heard out of you since we met."

Eitel winked back but Robert could see the worry in his face.

The rest of the afternoon, Robert finished Eitel's instruction on the reaper. For a while, Robert walked behind the machine, but he eventually got too tired and hopped into the gathering wagon to supervise from there. By this time, they had put Herr Dorsch's horses in the harnesses and although one of them pinned his ears back tight the whole time, they didn't panic at the noise from the reaper.

The sun was low when they spotted Gese running toward them, her skirts held in one hand. Robert, fearing the worst, hopped off the wagon and walked toward her. Eitel stopped the reaper and looked over at them.

He didn't need Eitel's translation. Lester had asked Gese to go get him. After quick instructions to the women on what to do with the horses and rig, Robert and Eitel hopped on the wagon and headed back to Eitel's farmhouse.

If anything, Lester looked even worse. *White as a sheet*, Robert's mom would have said.

"How ya feeling, bud?"

Lester spoke, but barely above a whisper. "I'm hanging, man."

Gese and her father entered the room. He had his hat in his hand and looked at Lester expectantly.

"I asked Gese to bring her father. I wanna know if he's gonna let her marry Eitel now."

Eitel flushed red.

"Lester, I don't think—" Robert began.

Lester raised a hand slightly. "I don't have the breath to waste. Ask him. Wait, no. *Tell* him I'm giving Eitel the reaper. He can make a good living with it, I think."

With Eitel's help, Robert translated. Gese began to cry as she absorbed the words. Heinrich grimaced and explained for a couple of minutes.

Robert heard him out and turned to Lester. "Correct me if I got that wrong, Eitel, but I think he apologized for saying no the first time. He says your gift isn't necessary and thanks us for all the help. He says you have saved the village."

Eitel nodded his head in agreement.

"Well. I'm giving it anyway. I guess I should've asked you first, Robert, but I'm pretty sure you don't mind."

"Course not. It was just a toy to us. But it's a godsend for them."

"Settled then. Robert, you been a good friend."

"You just shut up with that kind of talk. Get some sleep, and we'll see how you feel."

Gese made everyone leave except Robert, who pulled a chair up beside Lester's door. It was several hours later when Robert realized Lester's soft snoring had stopped. He quietly went to the bed and checked him for any sign of breathing. Wiping away tears, Robert crossed Lester's hands over his chest. He put his own hand on top of them. After a long while, he patted Lester, rose, found Belle, went to his own bed, and let exhaustion take him.

When Robert woke, it was nearly mid-morning. He heard careful moving sounds in the house and found Gese and a couple of the other women. Gese came over and embraced him briefly. The other women murmured words he did not understand but he could hear the sympathetic tone. He looked in the door to Lester's room but did not go in. Gese was saying something to him. After a moment, he realized she was saying they would make Lester ready. He nodded. He really didn't want to hang around the house and mourn. Gese found a girl to take him to where Eitel was working in a smaller field on the other side of the village. When the crowd there saw him, they gathered around him. Heinrich grabbed him by an arm and said something. Eitel translated.

"We are all so very sorry, Herr Butcher. We will never forget him or you. And the gift. We cannot repay such kindness. How can we help you?"

"I'll be fine. I intend to help you finish the harvest and then head home." He brushed off Eitel's objections. "I'd feel better doing something. And I'd like you to have the mules and wagon to go with the rig. Devil would never forgive me if I parted you two." They settled on Eitel driving him back to Grantville and returning with the wagon. That night they buried Lester beside Eitel's family. There were no clergy available, so they did what they could. Heinrich read from his Bible. Robert couldn't think of much more to say than *I loved you, brother.*

* * *

Two weeks after he got back to Grantville, they did a memorial service for Lester there. He didn't go because Lester's son, Guy, was mad and blamed him for Lester's death, even though Doc Adams told him it was inevitable. Guy made a little noise about pressing charges, but it really wasn't clear that anything was done illegally, so the matter was dropped. Robert decided he would go back to keeping to himself.

The morning after the memorial service, Robert was back on his porch rocking slowly. Belle took a nap on his bed. He had decided it was time to let go of Deanna's rules. In his hand was a letter Eitel had left him before taking the wagon and the mules back to his village. Robert kept thinking about one thing Eitel wrote. *Because you decided to help, everything has changed for me. And my people.* He folded the letter and put it in an envelope. With a grunt, he got up, grabbed some things from inside, and called to Belle. "Come on, girl, we're going into town."

He rode his bike, and Belle ran happily along. It was a bit of a hike to the Church of the Nazarene. Inside, the Red Cross folks were organizing care packages in the fellowship hall. He stood for a while in the doorway, not knowing what to do. Luckily, Kathryn Riddle was there, spotted him, and walked over.

"Well, Robert Butcher. I was wondering if you might take me up on my suggestion one day."

"Yeah. Well. I figured I could be of some use. And I thought I should be sharing this." He handed her a large paper bag. She took it, a slight frown on her face, and slowly opened the bag. Kathryn peered inside, smiled at him, then put her face in the bag and inhaled the scent.

"Oh, Robert. You're about to get very popular here. Come on in."

* * *

Assiti Shards

Into The Dark

Iver P. Cooper

An Alexander Inheritance Story

Queen of the Sea
In the Atlantic Ocean, en route to Trinidad
Early November, 321 BCE

"David Palacio, report to the staff captain." The loudspeaker announcement didn't say "immediately," but that was understood. The staff captain was the second-highest ranking officer on a cruise ship, and he headed the deck department.

"Guess you're in trouble," said Eric, an able seaman. He continued munching on a sandwich.

"Big trouble," added Giorgio, a plumber. "Or you'd be reporting to the chief carpenter. Or maybe the hotel services engineer, if the problem was in passenger accommodations." He slurped from his drink.

David gulped down the rest of his meal. "I have no idea what I did wrong." He didn't question the assumption that he was in trouble.

He put his tray where it belonged and left the deck crew cafeteria.

* * *

As he made his way to the staff captain's office, David wondered just what the issue might be. As one of the ship's carpenters, one of his duties was cleaning the woodworking shop on particular days of the week. Had he failed a subsequent inspection? That seemed more like something that the chief carpenter would call him to task for. Not the staff captain.

Had the potable water filling equipment failed? That was a carpentry responsibility, a holdover from sailing ship days, when the carpenter was in charge of the water barrels. Or had a wooden handrail given way, injuring a passenger?

It was with these dark thoughts swirling in his mind that he arrived at the staff captain's office.

* * *

When he opened the door, his qualms intensified. Staff Captain Anders Dahl was accompanied by Sherry whatever-her-surname-was, Sherry from Human Resources.

For an HR person to be present, perhaps as a witness, suggested that he had committed a disciplinary offense. Perhaps even a firing offense.

He took a deep breath, and said, "David Palacio, Carpenter, reporting, sir."

Dahl invited David to sit down and pulled a piece of paper out of a file. "Your resume lists 'caving' as one of your hobbies."

'Aye aye, sir."

"How long have you been caving?"

"Since I was thirteen, when my uncle took me to my first wild cave."

"You're from the Philippines?"

"Aye aye, sir."

"Lot of caves there?"

"Thousands. Including some of the biggest in the world. Some with underground rivers or lakes."

"Have you been caving elsewhere?"

"Lots of places. I take a cruise ship job, my room and board and medical are covered, so I get to save up money, and I use my free airfare 'home' to go someplace with caves. I go caving until I'm low in money, and then it's back on a cruise ship. It's a sweet life."

"What about in the Caribbean?"

"On Jamaica. I was hoping to go back at the end of this contract, but . . ." He shrugged.

"What do you know about black powder?"

"Just that it used to be used in firearms. And I think it's still used for fireworks."

"Well, you know that some of the Mediterranean powers have been casting covetous eyes at the *Queen*. We have had to use some of our up-time ammo to fend them off. That's a limited resource, and we are going to need to make more before we run out. It's easier to make black powder than the more modern propellants. The passengers and your fellow crewmen are counting on you to help make that happen."

"What can I do to help, sir?"

"We need three components for black powder: saltpeter, charcoal, and sulfur. Saltpeter is potassium nitrate. We've been able to buy saltpeter and sulfur in Alexandria and Tyre, but we can't count on them to always be available. Soon every would-be emperor will be making their own gunpowder.

"We've been very cautiously making gunpowder on board, but once we're in Trinidad, we want to move gunpowder production to the new colony. The gunpowder mill will want to obtain as many of the ingredients locally as possible. If not on Trinidad, then somewhere in the Caribbean.

"We've done some research in the archived Wikipedia, and it turns out that during the American Civil War, the Confederacy made saltpeter from bat guano. We have people with chemical backgrounds looking into just how to do that, but it doesn't do any good until we find the bat guano."

"And that's where I come in," David thought aloud.

"That's right. By the way, we need guano that's stayed dry. The reference material says water washes out the nitrates. Although I would guess that's more of an issue for seabird guano than bat guano. I don't suppose you know where there are bat caves on Trinidad?"

"Probably not," said David. "I do have stuff on my laptop about caves on Jamaica. There's even a Jamaica Caves Organization that I have gotten literature from. But even when a guidebook gives a location for a cave entrance, it can easily be a hundred yards off. Maybe more. And of course, the entrances that existed in the twenty-first century might not have opened up yet."

"But you can find caves?"

"Well, typically you find out about them from hunters or farmers who live in the immediate area. So that's who you need to ask first. If you want to find a solution cave, you want an area where you see limestone outcrops. You can follow streams and look for places where they disappear and resurface. Also, look for areas of heavy erosion. You can also watch for bats to see where they fly from at sunset or to at sunrise."

"It sounds like you know your stuff," said the staff captain approvingly. "What do you need to get on the project?"

"First, I need more cavers. The minimum team for wild caving is three, so two can carry out an injured caver. And if there aren't any on board, I'll have to train them."

Dahl looked at Sherry and then back at David. "You were the only employee who listed caving on his resume. We have circulated a questionnaire to the passengers, but it will take time to get answers."

"If there aren't any other cavers, then check for people who have done rock climbing. Or who are physically active and have jobs that take them into tight, enclosed spaces. We definitely don't want anyone who is claustrophobic, or who isn't physically fit."

"I'll make a note of that," said Sherry.

"There's equipment I'll need, too."

"Make a list, and I'll see what we can come up with," said Dahl. "In the meantime . . . Dismissed!"

INTO THE DARK

December, 321 BCE
On the *Queen of the Sea*, anchored off Trinidad

David looked over the would-be cavers that Sherry had sent to him. As he expected, the crew members were mostly in their twenties and thirties, and the passengers were mostly middle-aged. According to the dossiers that Sherry had provided, a few had rock climbing experience, and the rest had said that they liked to hike.

David had deliberately arranged for them to meet him in one of the larger interior rooms.

"Have any of you been wild caving before?"

There was silence.

"Have any of you been in show caves? By that I mean caves with stairs and electric lights."

Several of the passengers had.

"Did they ever turn out the electric lights?"

They shook their heads.

"Move away from the walls." David waited for his students to comply and then turned off the light. The room was now pitch-black.

"This is how much natural light you get in a cave once you're far enough away from the entrance. Let's just wait like this for a while."

After a few minutes he said, "How are you feeling? Panicky? Peaceful?"

"Maybe a little of both," someone answered. "It helps that I can hear everyone else breathing, to know that I am not alone. But wouldn't we have a light with us?"

"Sure. But batteries die, and torches get blown out or run out of fuel. When that happens, you have to be able to find your backup light and turn it on."

David flipped on the room lights. "Wild caving can be strenuous and dangerous. There will be times that you are crawling through tight spaces, making ascents or descents, or skirting pits. The point of doing exercises is to reduce the risk of injury and give you confidence in your abilities. The exercises you will be working on are to improve your balance, agility, stamina, flexibility, and upper body strength. Especially finger strength.

"We will do a few exercises together, so I have a sense of where you stand, but mostly you'll be working with the exercise room coaches, who have all sorts of equipment. I have given them your names and told them what's important for caving.

"Let's look at your balance first. You may find yourself on a narrow ledge, or even a rock bridge.

"There are chairs along the side of the room. Each of you take one. I want you to balance on one leg, then let go of the top of the chair. The chair is there so you have something to grab if you are starting to fall but I am hoping you don't need it. Try to hold position for thirty seconds. First on one leg, then on the other. And if you can hold position with the free foot raised underneath, try again but raise it forward. You can spread your arms out."

After they did this for a while, he brought out a wooden box and had them do step ups and step downs, first forward and backward and then side to side. Then he had them do jump ups and jump downs.

"That's enough for today. We'll meet again in a week and in the meantime be sure to go to the exercise room to get your coaching."

* * *

David made a deep dive into the ship's Wikipedia archive, to see what it had about caves on Trinidad. There were some promising hits. The Tamana caves were on the northern slope of Mount Tamana, which was in the eastern part of the Central Range. Eleven bat species permanently roosted in the cave. The Lopinot Cave was in the Lopinot Valley of the Northern Range and was home both to nocturnal oilbirds and to a large bat roost. The Aripo Cave was also in the Northern Range, in Tunapuna-Piarco district, and also home to oilbirds as well as bats. The Dunston Cave was an igneous cave in the Northern Range, containing an oilbird colony. The Cumaca Cave was in the southeastern area of the Northern Range, and it had bats, but since it also had catfish it couldn't be entirely dry. La Vache was in the Northern Range, on the north coast, and had oilbirds. There were several caves on the island Gaspar Grande, by the northwestern tip of Trinidad. There were also unnamed bat caves near the village of Paramin, in the western part of the Northern Range.

Hmm. The entry on the Northern Range mentioned, "Numerous sulfur springs occur on the riverbeds of Rio Seco Falls, demonstrating the volcanic nature of the region." Didn't the staff captain say that sulfur was an ingredient of gunpowder?

The Wikipedia search made it clear that it was unlikely that they would find any bat caves near Fort Plymouth, which was on the Gulf of Para on the west side of Trinidad.

Gaspar Grande was probably the best place to start searching, even though he didn't have any specific report of bats there. Since it was a small island—0.50 square miles—the area to be searched was limited.

Finding the other sites would be a lot harder. No global positioning satellites in the sky any more. But the *Queen* had found its way to Alexandria and Trinidad without GPS, so perhaps its navigation officers would have some suggestions.

* * *

Normally, the navigation officers of the *Queen* were very busy individuals. But not so much when the *Queen* was in port. David was able to get an appointment with Elise Beaulieu, first officer for navigation, without much trouble. He sent a note to the staff captain and next thing he knew, he was on her schedule.

"So, I have Google Earth location information for caves, but don't know how I can use it. I thought perhaps if I started at a known location—one the *Queen* had coordinates for—and kept my smartphone, that even without GPS it would tell me where I am."

Elise shook her head. "Afraid not. Or, more precisely, it would tell you a location, but it would be wrong, and the error would increase the farther you traveled. The low cost accelerometers, gyroscopes, and magnetometer-type compass built into a smartphone experience what we call 'drift.' I don't know offhand how much drift you would experience in walking, say, ten miles, but I'd be nervous about it. You could, I suppose, carry out a test—walk between two points of known coordinates, and see how far off it is."

"What about training me to use portable navigation instruments to determine my latitude and longitude?" asked David.

Elise sighed. "Assuming we had a sextant to spare—I'd have to ask the captain—it's still a bit tricky. The simplest way to determine latitude by observation is to wait until night and measure the altitude of the north star. However, Polaris isn't as close to the North Celestial Pole as it was in our time. So you have to correct for that. And for land navigation, measuring altitude is tricky because you don't have the flat horizon that we do at sea.

"As for measuring longitude, the most practical method is chronometer-based. I guess that you would be using a watch or smartphone as your chronometer. You set the chronometer to Greenwich time (or some other reference time for a known longitude) and see what time it reads at local noon. Local noon is when the sun reaches its highest point in the sky. It's not easy to tell exactly when that is, so we take two time readings, one a few minutes before local noon, when the sun is still ascending, and the other when it has descended back to the same altitude, and average the two.

"Here on the *Queen*, with sight reduction software corrected for the present day, we can do better, but I doubt that you could determine your longitude to better than a ten nautical mile accuracy. Your latitude error will be smaller, but still a mile or more.

"Given that Trinidad is about fifty miles from north to south and, up north where the staff captain said you'd be exploring, about sixty miles from west to east, I don't think celestial navigation will help you much."

She shrugged. "Sorry for the bad news."

* * *

When David met with the apprentice cavers again, he told them, "While there are caves that are big enough to hold concerts in, most of the time wild caves are on the small side. And even if the individual cave chambers are large, the passages between them may be pretty tight.

"When you were first recruited, the doctors checked that you had healthy hearts and that your girth was less than forty-two inches. While that means you are physically capable of crawling through a reasonably tight passage, it doesn't guarantee that you are free of claustrophobia. So, I have concocted a test. I'd like you all to try crawling through that." He pointed to a length of empty rectangular ventilation duct that he had positioned inside the room. The opening was ten inches tall and twenty-four inches wide.

One of the students studied it, and said, "Hah, I feel like I am auditioning for a heist movie."

Another joked, "Or I am on the starship *Enterprise* and I need to climb into a Jefferies tube."

David tapped his foot impatiently. "Whatever helps you actually do it, as opposed to talking about it."

They tried, one by one. "Fuck, this is uncomfortable," one complained. "I haven't crawled on my belly since I was a baby."

"Imagine how much fun it is to crawl along a tight tunnel that is inclined, so you have to struggle against gravity going up or brake going down. Or when the bottom is covered by water. Or cave cockroaches."

"You need to work on your pep talk," one of the students muttered.

* * *

The next day, it was more crawl practice. This time, David had them enter on their backs rather than on their bellies. Or crawl halfway in, with the room lights out, and just wait there until David gave them the go-ahead.

"I once did a crawl that was six hundred feet long, and took me about eight minutes to complete. So you need to be prepared for the possibility that you'll be in a tight space for a very long time."

One of the students started hyperventilating during this exercise, and David let him out early. "Do you want to try again?"

"Not really," he said.

"Well, thanks for trying."

Now there were only five apprentice cavers.

* * *

David still had the problem of finding the caves without combing through a hundred square miles of rough terrain. Perhaps the natives knew where the caves were. Perhaps they used them for refuge or created art in them or stored treasures. Or perhaps they ate bats.

While the caves that David knew about were either in the Northern Range—Akpara territory—or in the Central Range—Kapoi country—David thought it best to speak to Lacula, who traded with both groups and also was the native most familiar with the ship people.

David's first task was to make sure that Lacula knew what David meant by caves. He wanted a limestone cave, not a sea cave. David brought out his laptop and showed Lacula pictures of many different caves, pointing out the stalactites and stalagmites.

The next step was to convey the notion of bats. Wikipedia had a list of mammals of Trinidad and Tobago and there were a heck of a lot of links with photos in the section titled "order Chiroptera." Scores of them, actually.

Reading the descriptions, he realized there were plenty of bats in Trinidad that roosted in trees or in rock crevices rather than caves. That was going to be a problem insofar as locating bat caves was concerned. The best he could do, he decided, was to show Lacula pictures of the bats that seemed to prefer caves. Ghost-faced bats, Geoffroy's tailless bat, and Wagner's mustached bat, for example.

* * *

At Lacula's trading post, David said, "I want to find caves with bats in them. Dry caves, not sea caves. Are there any in the land of the Kaluga?"

Lacula shook his head. It was what David expected. While a lowland could still have sinkholes—Florida was notorious for them—Wikipedia had not mentioned any caves in southern Trinidad.

"What about in the lands of the Akpoka and the Kapoi?"

"There are certainly bats there," he said. "As for bat caves, I can find out." He rubbed his thumb and forefinger together and smiled.

"Yes, there will be a reward for you—if your informants lead us to a bat cave."

* * *

INTO THE DARK

The next day, any thoughts of bats were overshadowed by the news that one of the passengers, while trying to clear away growth for a farm, had been bitten just after sunset by a four-foot long pit viper.

A couple of Kaluga managed to kill the snake, and it was subsequently identified from Wikipedia photographs as a fer-de-lance, so called because its head was shaped like an iron lance or spearhead. More precisely, it was *Bothrops atrox*, called *mapepire balsain* on twenty-first century Trinidad.

The bitten passenger, who was about seventy years old, had to have his leg amputated just below the knee.

The fer-de-lance was a major topic of conversation at the next caving skills practice.

"Wikipedia says that *Bothrops* vipers are responsible for more fatalities in the Americas than any other group of venomous snakes," said one caving apprentice.

"That poor guy was bitten around sunset," offered another. "Isn't that when we would be looking for bats flying out of the caves?"

David had been researching the fer-de-lance, too. He found in the ship's electronic library a copy of Douglas Preston's *The Lost City of the Monkey God*. It said that the fer-de-lance comes out mostly at night, is attracted to people and activity, and is irritable and aggressive. It can spray venom six feet away, and its fangs can penetrate even the thickest leather boot.

"I'm not from here," said David, "but in the Philippines, there are plenty of venomous snakes. We have sea snakes, coral snakes, pit vipers, spitting cobras, and even the king cobra. I'll make sure that we have snake gaiters. They give additional protection from the instep to just below the knee." David refrained from quoting Preston's comment that the fer-de-lance sometimes leaps upward when it strikes, hitting above the knee.

"We will also have lanterns so we can see what's on the trail ahead of us. You can carry a walking stick to probe the ground ahead of you. And we will sleep in hammocks." He paused. "And if you need to go pee, look below you first."

January, 320 BCE
Fort Plymouth

"You must be David Palacio, the caver."

David turned. He was being addressed by one of the passengers. Very attractive, and well dressed to boot. That wasn't common on Fort Plymouth, given the heat and humidity. It suggested that she worked someplace with air conditioning.

"How could you tell?" David smiled. He was wearing a hard hat with an LED light attached and carrying a coil of rope. He was just returning from a practice session with his student cavers.

She gave him a fifty-kilowatt smile, which made him a bit suspicious. "I'm Amanda Miller, assistant to President Wiley."

"I have heard of you."

Before the Event, since he was a carpenter, a lot of his work was in the passenger cabins and hallways. His conversations with them had been on the order of "Good morning" and "Excuse me." Fraternization with passengers had been discouraged. Since the Event that had changed somewhat, but there were four thousand passengers, and he certainly didn't know all of them. Amanda, however, had played a prominent role in Wiley's campaign to be President of New America, as Trinidad was now called. Even the parts that the natives hadn't actually ceded to the ship people.

"Could we talk in private, please?"

David shrugged and pointed. "We can go under that tree."

"Great." Once they were situated, Amanda went into her spiel.

"The gunpowder mill is owned fifty-fifty by the Queen of the Sea Corporation and the government of New America."

"Okay . . ."

"But the mill gets its saltpeter from the Queen of the Sea Corporation, and they charge a lot for it. They say it is because they have to import it from the Mediterranean, and the countries that have it keep raising their prices, as they are making their own gunpowder. They say the only reason they can still get it is because the Egyptians figure that if they don't sell to the *Queen*, the Carthaginians will, and so on.

"Now, one way of making saltpeter is by processing human waste. That's how it was done in England, say. But we don't have the population base to have a lot of that. And it takes time for the niter beds to mature." She involuntarily wrinkled her nose.

"Since some of your apprentice cavers are passengers, I know that the *Queen* is planning to have you find bat caves on Trinidad, to give it a domestic supply of saltpeter. But they haven't said a word about sharing the benefit of that supply with New America."

David squirmed. "I'm a full-time employee of the *Queen*."

"Yes, and you are being paid a carpenter's salary to do something that no one else on this island can do. We—meaning the government of New America—have a much greater appreciation of your value. If you were to do cave exploration for us instead, we'd be willing to show our appreciation in a very tangible way. You wouldn't just get a salary, you'd be given royalties on the production from the caves you discovered."

"I'll . . . I'll have to think about it."

"Do that. To give us clear title to your discoveries, you'll need to resign from the *Queen* and be under contract to us before you find any bat caves. And as a practical matter, that means you need to make a decision before the *Queen* heads back to the Mediterranean. Which I believe will be happening next month."

* * *

The *Queen* was down-sizing, David knew. Before the Event, it had a crew of almost a thousand. Scuttlebutt had it that Human Resources was trying to cut that number in half. Moreover, David heard that they were trying to get rid of almost all of the original hotel staff, since they could get cooks, waiters, and so on more cheaply in Europe.

Strictly speaking, David was in the deck department, not in hotel services. But there wasn't a tremendous demand for carpenters on board a modern cruise ship. The cabins had wooden paneling, wooden handrails lined the internal corridors, and the promenade deck was wood, but the hull was metal.

It was true that a ship's carpenter worked in more than just wood; they also handled glass and aluminum. But there were glassworkers as well as carpenters for hire in Europe, and it would be awhile before anyone was producing aluminum.

David figured that the only reason he hadn't been involuntarily discharged to the colony was because of his caving skills. But what would happen to him once he found a bat cave with guano?

The deal from New America was sounding better and better.

* * *

The 150,000-ton *Queen of the Sea* was one of the largest cruise ships in the twenty-first century world it came from, and it therefore offered some unusual "at-sea" recreational activities. One of those was a climbing wall. The first cruise ship with a climbing wall was Royal Caribbean's 1999 *Voyager of the Seas*, 137,000 tons. And a decade later, the 156,000-ton *Norwegian Epic* upped the ante with a rappelling wall.

Before the Event, David had not been able to try it out, as it had been reserved for guests. Once he was given the task of training a caving team, he quickly realized that it should be incorporated into the program. Southwest Trinidad, where Fort Plymouth was situated, was rather flat and thus offered little opportunity to learn climbing skills.

David called his students to attention. "I know that there are a couple of experienced rock climbers among you, and I hope you will help the others.

"This is a good, safe place to begin learning climbing skills, but bear in mind that here you don't have to worry that the rock you are holding onto will give way. Or that a climber above you might dislodge a rock. And the *Queen*'s wall isn't slippery, either, as walls in caves often are.

"Given the climate here on Trinidad, we are going to be sweating a lot, which makes it harder to maintain a good hold on even a dry cliff face. Unfortunately, I don't think we have a lot of climbing chalk available. Back in the Philippines, we used dry dirt or sand, or crushed dry leaves."

The *Queen* had an employee who served as the rock climbing wall instructor and guard, and David let him explain how to use the climbing harnesses and ropes (some of which would be commandeered by David, as authorized by the staff captain). The team tried out several routes, which varied in difficulty.

Once they were all back at the base of the wall, David congratulated them on their progress.

One of the students raised his hand. "I am not sure why we need climbing skills. The whole point is to mine bat guano, right? We aren't going to have miners go up and down ropes every day."

"Good question," said David. "If we find bat guano, an evaluation will be made of how difficult it is to access, and whether we can make that access easier. We can install ladders or build stairs or hoists. Whether it is worth it or not depends on the depth and how much guano is there. But the first step is to find the guano, and for that, we need to be able to climb if need be."

* * *

David brooded about an essential set of skills that he had not been able to teach: the ones used for climbing in confined spaces. While they might descend a rope to enter a cave system, once they were inside, chimneying, stemming. and bridging would probably prove more useful. All three techniques involved bracing oneself between two walls and using pressure to move vertically or horizontally.

Some athletic centers that David had visited had climbing walls with special spelunking sections, where two walls nearly met. You could practice chimneying there, but the *Queen*'s climbing wall was of a simpler type.

Some of the passageways on the *Queen* were three feet wide and seven feet high. That was theoretically suitable for practicing horizontal movement in a chimney. But the flat walls made it tricky, as there were no footholds or handholds.

It looked like David's students would have to just follow his lead when they encountered a chimney in a cave.

* * *

David and his team pushed a Zodiac into the water of the Gulf of Paria, near modern San Fernando, and clambered aboard. The helmsman started up the outboard motor and they chugged off. The Zodiac could easily go sixty miles per hour but he kept it throttled down to conserve fuel. Even at reduced speed, they made it to Gaspar Grande in an hour.

The *Queen* did not have a complete Google Earth download but it did have full detail for the Caribbean, which was its expected theater of operation. This download included a georeferenced photo of "Gasparee Caves," on Gaspar Grande. The picture showed a large cave room with stalactites and stalagmites.

Gaspar Grande was nominally within Akpara territory, but the Akpara who came to Fort Plymouth doubted that it was inhabited, as it had no fresh water sources. As far as they knew, at least.

Google Earth showed that the island was about 1.5 miles long, west to east, and about half a mile wide, north to south. The dominant physical feature was a west-to-east ridge with three humps. If the georeference was accurate, the cave was on the westernmost hump, a little north of the ridge line.

The easiest access appeared to be from a little cove on the northwest side of the island. From there, if they walked in the correct direction, it should be a tenth of a mile. Unfortunately, the island was heavily forested. Finding the cave wasn't going to be easy.

They decided to head straight south from the cove and hope for the best. Progress was slow; they had to keep cutting undergrowth with their machetes. It eventually became apparent that they had crossed the ridge line and were descending toward the south side of the island. They had obviously overshot the cave. Assuming the georeferenced location was correct. And their compass was properly corrected for magnetic variation and deviation. And they had picked the correct course. And there was in fact an entrance to the cave in this century.

They decided to return to the ridge line and wait there until sunset. Hopefully, they would see bats, and they could judge the cave's location from the bats' flightpath.

* * *

They didn't see any bats. However, there was no lack of mosquitoes, which did their darndest to bite through the netting covering their faces and necks.

They made camp for the night.

INTO THE DARK

* * *

At sunrise, they did see bats . . . and they were flying in the opposite direction from the one expected. That is to say, south, over the ridge, instead of north.

That was annoying, to say the least. It took another couple of days of camping to actually find the cave. The bats flew out at sunset and returned at sunrise.

The cave was a large one. It wasn't completely dark because there was a series of surface sink holes above. (The team had roped down through one of them.) At the bottom of the cave was a saltwater lagoon. There were fish-eating bats, but obviously, their guano was feeding the fish, so the cave couldn't be mined.

"Very pretty," said David, "and perhaps in fifty years, we'll have stairs, electric lights, and tourists to overcharge. But insofar as the gunpowder mill is concerned, this is a dud."

* * *

David still had to make a decision about the New America offer. He definitely didn't want to antagonize the staff captain on the *Queen* by getting in the middle of the sometimes fraught relations between the *Queen* and New America.

While New America's offer to David sounded good, David wondered what would happen once he found the guano. Would they want him to keep looking for additional caves, or would it be, "Thanks, go find someone who needs a carpenter."

David decided he needed to up his game and figure out what value caves might have once modern gunpowder replaced black powder. He did some research and it appeared that the most obvious point was that bat guano could be used as a fertilizer. Moreover, it appeared that saltpeter, besides being used to make gunpowder, could also be used as a bluing agent, a preservative, a thickening agent, and an anti-asthma and hypotensive medication.

He kept digging and found out that cave silt contains actinomycetes and molds that might secrete antibiotics, and dried "moonmilk," a claylike cave material used in the sixteenth and seventeenth centuries as a wound dressing. As for cave minerals, gypsum was used to make white body paint, and mirabilite and epsomite for food seasoning. Finally, caves had been used for mushroom growing and cheese aging, and cave air could air condition buildings. David wasn't sure that the latter uses would be practical in Trinidadian caves, since cave temperatures increased as latitude decreased.

Hopefully, that was enough to make sure that New America would be willing to keep a caver on their payroll, long-term.

With this literary ammunition in hand, he sought out Amanda Miller and got a contract from New America, on better terms than those offered initially, to start upon his resignation from the *Queen*.

* * *

By this point, the *Queen* had a formal schedule of payouts for resigning crew members, based on their department, rank, and seniority with the cruise line. Even so, they tried to talk him out of resigning, realizing that if he succeeded in his quest, New America would have an independent source for saltpeter. But they weren't willing to match New America's offer.

Of course, that put the onus of equipping the caving expedition on New America.

"So what's needed?" asked Amanda warily.

"For orienteering, we will need compasses, machetes, at least one pair of binoculars, and some sort of waterproof writing gear. Clothing to protect us from insects, snakes, thorns, and rock scrapes. Stuff for marking a trail that won't quickly wear or blow away.

"For the actual caving, hard helmets, helmet-mounted lights, backup lights, knee and elbow pads, first aid kit, knives, whistles, and ropes. Climbing harnesses and associated gear, like tensioners, too. With fewer passengers on board, there are going to be fewer people making use of the *Queen*'s climbing wall.

"Bear in mind that I already asked the staff captain to get all that equipment when I was working for the *Queen*. Hopefully, he will loan or sell it to New America."

"Leave that to me," said Amanda.

INTO THE DARK

Lacula had put out feelers as to whether any of the natives had come across bat caves. But that didn't mean that he hired messengers to go to every Akpara and Kapoi village. That would have been expensive, and he hadn't been offered any up-front payment. No, as Akpara and Kapoi came to his trading post, he brought up the subject and asked them to spread the word. So news of the ship people's interest in bat caves disseminated slowly, along the coast and up the rivers.

According to Wikipedia, the biggest concentration of known caves was in the Northern Range. David thought the easiest of those caves to find would probably be Lopinot Cave. He had compared the Google Earth imagery to a Wikipedia map of Trinidad that showed watercourses. That showed that the Caroni River could be followed upstream, eastward. According to the Google Earth imagery, counting from the mouth, the fifth tributary coming down from the north was the one David wanted. It was called the Oropuna, and before it came the San Juan, the Saint Joseph, the Tunapuna, and the Macoya.

Heading upstream on the Oropuna, he would take the "second stream left," the Arouca, and continue northward, passing close to the up-time village of Lopinot. (At some point, presumably, it became the Lopinot River.) According to Wikipedia, a plantation was established there in the early nineteenth century because it was flat land in the midst of mountainous terrain. Perhaps the Akpara had settled it for the same reason?

Google Earth showed a georeferenced photo of an entrance to "Lopinot Cave" a short distance upstream of the village, and being able to follow a river would be a big advantage in terms of finding the place.

Of course, the Google Earth photography showed the northern Trinidad of the early twenty-first century, not the fourth century BCE. River courses could change considerably over twenty-three hundred years. Moreover, even if the imagery was accurate in the here-and-now, this was the dry season, and they might overlook one of the tributaries if it was dried out.

Also, unfortunately, the land flanking the Caroni River was flat, and, looking at a simulated view of the Northern Range from the confluence with the fifth tributary, there was no obvious landmark they could use as a reference.

David had created a waterways sketch map based on the Google Earth data, and explained it to Lacula. Hopefully, he would explain it in turn to his Akpara contacts, and they would know what turn-offs David's expedition needed to make.

* * *

Lacula found an Akpara in Fort Plymouth who was the brother of one who had married into an Akpara village somewhere up the Caroni. Lacula believed that this village was in the vicinity of the mouth of the fourth tributary, the Macoya, and thus not far from the desired turn off.

The Akpara visitor was confident he could lead David's party to his brother's new village. He didn't know anything about bat caves, there or elsewhere, but Lacula nonetheless pressed David for a "finder's fee." David referred him to Amanda, who paid him off. Of course, the Akpara would also be hired as a guide.

* * *

It still bothered David that he was so reliant on native knowledge, and the accuracy of Lacula's communications with the Akpara, to find the correct tributary. He knew the distance from the mouth of the Caroni to that tributary in Google Earth. Could he use that?

Elise had warned him that dead reckoning by use of his smartphone would be inaccurate because of drift—integration errors. And unless he had a solar charger, the smartphone would run out of juice before he reached his destination. An ordinary pedometer wouldn't work if he was on a boat. He did some investigating, and found out that in the mid-nineteenth century, there was something called the "patent log," a vaned rotor towed behind the ship.

That was something that, as a carpenter, he thought he could build. And he could correct to some degree for the effect of river current by measuring how many turns it made in a set period when he held it at a fixed point in the river, using a long fishing pole, perhaps. And if he didn't have a working watch or smartphone, he could use a sand timer.

* * *

New America had acquired several of the *Queen*'s all-weather lifeboats, since the *Queen* was going to carry fewer passengers from now on. The boats were equipped with engines, folding mast and sail, and oars.

Two were assigned to David's expedition, the *Miss Anne* and the *Miss Betty*. One carried David, his caving team, and their equipment, and the other their native support group—interpreters, porters, a cook, and guards. Prudently, both boats carried food and drinking water.

They sailed from Fort Plymouth to the Akpara village at the mouth of the Caroni River. As Lacula had warned them, they had to work their way through a mangrove swamp and then over a sandbar.

The village buildings were round huts, not unlike Lacula's trading post, arranged in a circle. Since it was the dry season, there didn't appear to be much activity in the nearby fields. Dogs barked at the expedition members as their native guide led them into the village. The Akpara guide found his brother's hut and brought him out to meet the visitors. David presented gifts to him.

The brother then took him to meet the First Man of the village. This warranted a further presentation of gifts. The First Man urged David to switch to dugout canoes. It was now the middle of the dry season, and the lifeboats weren't likely to make it far upriver. The skippers of the *Miss Anne* and *Miss Betty* said that they would return to Fort Plymouth but would revisit the mouth of the Caroni in May, or earlier if they received a message that they should do so.

While some of the Akpara canoes had sails, those weren't going to help them. Trinidad was in the northeast trade wind belt, and that meant that the wind would be against them.

As the expedition poled its canoes up the Caroni, David couldn't help but notice how high the banks were above the present water level. It was a sign of what they could expect come June, when the rainy season began.

When they made camp the first night on the Caroni, David watched the scarlet ibises, hundreds strong, returning from Venezuela to their roosts in the mangrove swamp to the south.

It was one of the most remarkable sights David had seen in all the time he had spent in the wilds of the world.

Lopinot Region, Trinidad

David's party was passed on, from one village to another, until they found one where the residents had knowledge of bat caves. David didn't know for sure whether the village they had been guided to was in the vicinity of modern Lopinot, but he thought it likely. The distance traveled, based on his patent log, seemed about right, and this was a flat space in a mountainous region.

The cave that the Lopinoteans led David to was a sloped hill. The entrance was of a moderate size. David and his cavers entered it single file. Pillars of limestone flanked the entrance, and they were green with algae. They worked their way around some large blocks and found themselves in a chamber about twenty feet long. There were several knee-high stalagmites.

"Do you smell something?" asked one of the cavers. "Like ammonia cleaner?"

"You're smelling bat urine," said David. "That's a good sign."

They studied the walls and roof, but didn't see anything. "I can't hear them either," one added.

David had told them that the sounds that bats make to navigate and find prey—the echolocation sounds—were pitched too high for humans to hear. (He had hoped that one of the electrical engineers on the *Queen* could build him a bat detector, but they had been way too busy.) What you could hear unaided were the social communication sounds: pups asking to be fed, male bats seeking a mate, or fighting bats insulting each other.

They moved deeper into the cave, and, in the center of the chamber, they found bats. They were roosting in a ceiling pit. David pointed them out to his cavers.

"What kind of bat are they?" someone whispered.

"I am not sure," said David. "We'd have to catch one, and then I'd have to look it up in my guide. Bats are usually identified by their echolocation calls, but for that I'd need an acoustic bat detector, and I don't have one."

"How many do you think are up there?"

David shrugged. "A few hundred." He brought his lantern close to the floor and studied it. "But what's important is we're walking on compacted guano."

The cavers took out tools and bagged samples of the guano from different parts of the cave and different depths below the surface.

"Are we all set?" asked David. "Okay, let's continue."

At the back of the chamber another, rather narrow passageway sloped downward. David crawled in, belly down.

The passageway was perhaps five feet long and led down into a larger cave. While the upper cave had a relatively flat floor, this one was more of an inverted cone. Here the slope deepened to about forty-five degrees. David called for a weighted rope to be brought down to him. Once he had the rope in hand, his assistant backed up the passageway with the aid of the rope (and, when he got far enough up-slope, yet another caver pulled the assistant up by his feet).

Here, he used his LED headlamp. (He had made only sparing use of this, because there were only so many batteries in Fort Plymouth.) It appeared that there was guano here, too, but looser. He took a couple of samples, and then headed back up.

"We're done for the day, let's head back to the village."

"And do we start heading back to our rendezvous point tomorrow?"

David shook his head. 'The cave is dry right now, but we don't know what it's like when it rains. If water flows over the guano, that's bad, it will leach out the nitrates. The guano will still be good as fertilizer, but that's not what we're looking for right now."

"So we want a cave that's dry year-round."

"Well, no running water under the bat roosts," David qualified. "It's okay if there's a slow seep—that's what keeps the stalactites and stalagmites growing—since then the dissolved nitrates don't travel far before the water evaporates. In fact, seeping water might be a good thing, as the nitrates will precipitate out as a white powder."

* * *

David's expedition spent a month with the Lopinoteans and explored three more caves in the area. They had to access Lopinot Cave #2 by a crawl space that was just sixteen inches high, and because the entrance was so narrow, the chamber beyond was in essentially total darkness. Nonetheless, they were rewarded with dry chambers containing thousands of bats and a floor covered with dry bat guano. Unfortunately, the guano had also attracted a large number of giant cockroaches, and it was unpleasant just walking in the chambers. Everyone was glad that they didn't have to crawl where the insects were feasting.

They entered Lopinot Cave #3 by a fifteen-foot sinkhole with a talus cone at the bottom. The sinkhole walls had handholds and footholds enough to be climbable, but David deemed it best to play it safe and carry out a rope descent. The sinkhole was connected to several additional chambers. Bats were plentiful, as was guano, but the drip rate after it had rained for two days was high. They took guano samples anyway.

The final cave, Lopinot Cave #4, was a walk-in. There was a small colony of bats, and some guano, but David was skeptical that this cave would prove of value as there were signs of water through-flow.

Fort Plymouth
May, 320 BCE

It was May—nearly the end of the dry season—when David's expedition returned to Fort Plymouth.

"So when will we know whether the bat guano is any good?" asked David.

"Soon," said Amanda. "We have a chemist working on recreating something called the Kjeldahl method for nitrogen analysis. And from that we can calculate the potential saltpeter yield."

"Why didn't you have that done while I was training my team or gallivanting around northern Trinidad?"

"Because we are short of everything. Short on chemists, short on equipment, short on raw materials. The only real chemist in Fort Plymouth right now—that is, one who worked as a chemist before the Event—has a dozen projects, all needed yesterday. For a nitrogen assay, I was told, we needed to make sulfuric acid, potassium sulfate, sodium hydroxide, hydrochloric acid, and pH indicator dye, in known concentrations, and find the right catalyst for the conversion of amine nitrogen into ammonium ions. We also needed to make the lab glassware. Bear in mind that the *Queen* didn't have a chemistry laboratory, and we lost access to most of its resources when it sailed back to Europe. The assay was low priority until you came back with the guano."

"So be it," said David. "What should I do in the meantime? Plan an expedition to the Mount Tamana region?"

Amanda considered this suggestion. "Not just yet. Give your caving team a break, a chance to catch up with other stuff. And there's plenty of demand for your carpentry skills right now."

June, 320 BCE

The assay results for Lopinot Caves One and Two were quite favorable. The colony's chemist estimated that they would be able to make on average at least four pounds of saltpeter from every hundred pounds of guano. The guano from Cave Three produced only half that quantity. And the guano from Cave Four was suitable only for fertilizer, which was a pity, as it had the easiest access.

The next step was for David to guide Samuel Leadbetter, a passenger who had owned his own construction firm, to the cave. He would be in overall charge of the guano mining operation, among other projects. He needed to see the caves in order to decide what site modifications were needed for guano mining to be practical—assuming it could be made practical at all.

Both caves had passageways that would need to be enlarged, whether with explosives or with pick and shovel. David warned him that the demolition crew should wear respirators or masks, as fresh bat droppings might contain spores of the fungus *Histoplasma capsulatum*, and their work could send the spores airborne. Breathing in the spores could result in pneumonia-like histoplasmosis, known as "cave disease." David had no idea whether that fungus was present in Trinidad, but he wanted to make sure Sam knew about it.

Leadbetter also had to check the condition of the roof and floor—for hazards such as falling rock, or pits to trip and fall into. There needed to be adequate lighting without depleting the oxygen supply in the cave. And so on and so forth.

Unfortunately, by the time the chemist finished the assays of the guano samples, it was already June, and they were faced with torrential rains. No one wanted to travel far in the wild under those conditions. So they waited until December, when the rains were slacking off.

December, 320 BCE

Since they knew where they were going and the landmarks to watch out for, and water levels were high enough to use *Miss Anne* and *Miss Betty* while on the Caroni, this trip took less time.

They sounded out the Lopinoteans as to their willingness to mine guano and received a series of polite refusals. It wasn't a surprise. They would be working by lantern light in a confined space, with high temperature and humidity and an acrid smell from the guano.

Ship people were even less likely than the Akpoka to engage in guano mining. Almost certainly, the guano miners would be indentured servants, bought from the Suthic or the Carthaginians. Or criminals or prisoners sentenced to hard labor, although the legality of that was open to question.

January, 319 BCE

Plans for the guano mining were well underway when one of the ex-passengers knocked on the door of David's home. When he answered, she demanded to know, "Are you the idiot that is planning to despoil bat caves in the Northern Range?"

"It is true that I found bat caves . . ." David responded cautiously. "Who are you?"

"I am Anna Comfort, and I am the representative of Northern Trinidad in the Congress of New America. And I insist you cease this activity until a proper study of its environmental impact may be conducted."

"Actually, I am not involved in the guano mining. And in finding the caves, I acted under orders from President Wiley of New America."

"Acting under orders, huh?" Anna sniffed. "Where have we heard that before? Nazi Germany?"

David shook his head. "Look, you don't like the idea, you need to talk to President Wiley."

"Rest assured that I will."

* * *

David decided that he had better talk to Amanda Miller, to see if she could pull Anna's fangs.

"Excuse me, Miz Miller, but someone named Anna Comfort has been giving me a hard time about the guano mining project. She insists that we stop it so we don't hurt the bats."

"Anna Dis-Comfort, eh?" Amanda muttered. "She thinks she's the governor of Northern Trinidad, but she's just one of its representatives in Congress. I'll take care of her."

Something about David's reaction gave her pause. "What's wrong?"

"I know that the bat guano is a critical resource for making saltpeter and therefore gunpowder, but I do appreciate where she's coming from," said David. "In the Philippines, where I come from, there were over a hundred caves that were closed to the general public. Not just to protect the bats, but other wildlife, and also the geological formations."

"But there were still some caves that anyone could visit?" asked Amanda.

"Sure. There were at least forty that you could visit not just for the thrill, or to see the formations, but also to collect guano for fertilizer and bird's nests for soup."

"It sounds like in the Philippines that you had a lot more caves to choose from than we do in Trinidad. At least, caves we know about."

"That's true. Actually, we had a couple of thousand, but a lot of them hadn't been classified."

Amanda stroked her chin. "Okay, why don't you and Samuel Leadbetter sit down with Michael Lockwood? He's our go-to person for any environmental issues."

"We'll do that."

* * *

Lockwood leaned back in his chair. "David, I understand that you were a member of a Philippine caving organization. What environmental concerns were raised about people entering bat caves to harvest guano?"

"Lights and noise disturb bats. Smoke from torches can suffocate bats or set the guano on fire. And changes to the entrance might change the temperature and humidity in the cave in a way that the bats don't like."

"What was proposed to protect the bats?"

"First, if the bats are migratory, then harvest the guano when they're not around."

Lockwood made a note. "Do we know whether these bats are migratory?"

"No. There isn't much change in temperature in Trinidad, so if they are, it is probably because of a change in food supply associated with the change between the rainy and the dry seasons."

"'The bats eat insects, right?"

"It depends on the species. Some eat fruit. But both can vary with the season."

"The dry season is January to May, and that's when you first discovered the caves," said Lockwood. "The rainy season is June to December, and that's when you went back with George."

"Well, we waited until the end of the rainy season, but yes."

"And you saw the same bat population densities?"

"Pretty much, although we didn't take a count."

"Then I think we need to assume that these bats aren't migratory. So what's the next best option?"

"Almost all bats are nocturnal, even the fruit bats. They leave at sunset and return at sunrise. So do the harvesting when they are out on the prowl."

Lockwood turned to Leadbetter. "Is that feasible?"

"Well, we need light inside the cave even in the daytime, so sure."

"You need to wait to turn on the lights until all the bats have flown off," added David.

"Let me think," muttered Leadbetter. "Since we're in the tropics, the length of the day is almost constant, about twelve hours. Take off an hour on each end for bat transit, and that's ten hours, which is a pretty long work day."

"You're probably going to have people working an hour on, an hour off, that whole period," said David. "The conditions are oppressive."

"I suppose we can live with that."

'What about the issue of disturbing the bats when you change the access?" asked Lockwood.

"Do as little as you can get away with," suggested David.

"Suppose we were to enlarge the entrances but put in some sort of Dutch door, so that when the miners aren't at work, we leave just the top section open to mimic the natural condition?" asked Leadbetter. "We could even construct a sort of airlock, with Dutch doors at each end, if we had to."

David grimaced. "I am sure that would help reduce the impact on the bats, I just can't say how much."

Lockwood liked the idea anyway. "But what about the lighting? Can we avoid using lanterns and torches inside the caves?"

"Sure," grumbled Leadbetter, "if we want to use up our irreplaceable LED lights and batteries."

"We do have rechargeable batteries. Even some solar chargers," protested Lockwood. "And aren't the LED lights good for something like 25,000 hours? Even 50,000? By the time they die, we'll probably be able to make LEDs in this timeline."

"I am not sure I would make that assumption," said Leadbetter. "But aren't there some woods that burn with very little smoke? Ash, oak, maple . . ."

Lockwood cut him off. "Even if we find wood like that here, the problem isn't just the smoke, it's the depletion of oxygen and production of carbon dioxide that we need to worry about."

"And not just on account of the bats . . ."

* * *

Lockwood submitted an environmental impact statement to President Wiley who, "as a courtesy," shared it with Anna Comfort.

As feared and expected, she was not mollified and managed to persuade a committee of the Congress of New America to hold a hearing on the "impact of guano mining."

Anna Comfort was not the chair of the committee, and President Wiley had sufficient clout with the chair to make sure that the first panel was of people who would talk about the benefit of guano mining—the strategic advantage of having a domestic source of saltpeter for gunpowder manufacture and the economic value of even the discarded phosphate-rich material as fertilizer for crops.

Anna tried to argue that the contract between the Lopinoteans and the colony was unfair to the former. However, even the Akpara on the committee were unmoved. The Akpara thought of themselves more as a culture than as a nation or tribe. Each village was an independent polity. If the Lopinoteans didn't negotiate the best possible deal for themselves, then the rest of the Akpara simply didn't care. If anything, they were a little envious that the Lopinoteans had this resource and they didn't. Their concern was that the Lopinoteans not get a special deal on gunpowder. And the principal concern of the other franchised tribes—the Kapoi and the Kaluga—was that the Akpara in general didn't get a special deal on gunpowder.

Some of the ship people did want to make sure that the contract wasn't exploitative, but one of the witnesses explained that it was similar to the deals made for access to oil fields in southern Trinidad.

INTO THE DARK

David Palacio, Samuel Leadbetter, and Michael Lockwood were on the second panel of witnesses and from the beginning were treated by Anna as hostile witnesses. However, other congressmen were rather more sympathetic to the project.

The general attitude toward bats among the ship people was a mix of "bats are rats with wings," "bats are good because they eat mosquitoes," and "bats are blood suckers."

The Trinidadians were rather more knowledgeable about bats. Bats were found all over Trinidad, they just didn't live in caves in the south (because there weren't any). And there were two things that bothered them about bats: they ate wild fruit (that the Trinidadians would rather gather and eat themselves) and some species—yes, vampire bats—attacked people.

Their view was that it made sense to make some effort at protecting the bats so they would keep producing guano. But they weren't about to elevate the interests of bats over those of human beings.

Anna then pressed for a third panel, this time of medical people, to talk about the health risks to the miners. The panelists talked about histoplasmosis and also about the possible transmission of rabies by bats, especially vampire bats. There was a Wikipedia article reporting that white-winged vampire bats had transmitted rabies on modern Trinidad.

David was recalled to testify as to whether there were vampire bats in any of the caves that were earmarked for guano mining. He pointed out that no one in the expedition had been bitten by bats during their explorations and that the Wikipedia article on Lopinot cave said that the cave had been used to study the behavior of the Greater Spear-Nosed Bat and made no reference to vampire bats.

After the hearing, Anna Comfort introduced a bill to ban guano mining on Trinidad. It was voted down in committee.

* * *

Sometime later, David was buttonholed by Lacula, who was now a congressman. "You told me that your Wikipedia said that there were bat caves in central Trinidad, in Kapoi country?"

"That's right, on the north slope of Mount Tamana."

"Well, I have some Kapoi friends who would like you to go there. On their behalf."

"Is that going to get me in trouble with President Wiley?"

Lacula shook his head. "Oh, no. President Wiley is perfectly happy to entertain a proposal from the Kapoi where they share in the expenses of the expedition and the subsequent profits. Especially since it means that there will be competition with the Akpara."

David thought about what he had read about the bat caves of Mount Tamana. It was supposed to be an eighteen-section cave system, with eleven different bat species permanently roosting in the caves. There was supposed to be a subterranean stream, too, but some cave areas were dry. It sounded like Paradise to a caving enthusiast like himself.

"Well, then . . . Mount Tamana, here I come!"

* * *

State Library Papers

Farm Equipment
That Came Through
the Ring of Fire
By George Grant

Farm Equipment That Came Through the Ring of Fire

George Grant

If those who came through the Ring of Fire had any higher priority than defending themselves, it can only have been providing enough food. To that end, they needed and continue to need appropriate farm equipment. This article will elucidate what equipment they likely had upon arrival, based on a recent visit to Mannington.

On the way to the 2021 Capclave/RoFCon, Jack Carroll and I stopped in Mannington for two days. While there we visited the Round Barn Museum and drove perhaps half of the rural roads within the Ring, looking at the land and the farm equipment. We also spoke with some of the long-time residents. The results were quite revealing.

What we saw was there in 2021, not 2000. But much of the equipment we saw was made before 2000, and besides tending to be conservative, farmers generally can't afford to buy new equipment if the old will continue to serve. Even in those cases where a piece of equipment is newer, it most likely replaced a similar older piece. Farmers know what they can and cannot do with their land, and the land hasn't changed. Equipment that was suitable to work the land in 2000 is still suitable now. Given the slow abandonment of farmland over the years, there was likely more equipment in 2000 than there is now.

The most surprising results came from an unexpected source. Jack wanted to visit the machine shops, so just as he rode along with me to look at the farms, I went into the shops with him. While he was quizzing one employee, I chatted with another. He told me he had grown up putting up loose hay and farming with horses—and he was only in middle age.

Apparently, the age of horse-powered agriculture lasted quite a bit longer there than I would ever have expected. He said some farmers were still working that way into the 1970s. He also said that in the year 2000, the majority of horses in the area were still work horses and used in work competitions. He estimated perhaps twenty teams would compete annually at the fair. We can expect that to resume down-time once the farmers have the time.

His most surprising datum, though, was the number of horse-drawn implements he estimated were still there in 2021—and I did specify within three miles of Mannington. He thought there were at least six hundred to one thousand pieces, thirty to forty percent in usable condition, and the rest restorable. Given there are bound to be pieces hidden away he is unaware of, I lean toward the high side of his estimate. Projecting back to 2000, there were likely over a thousand, and it seems reasonable to assume around half would have still been operable.

Specifics

The horse-drawn equipment we actually saw included a carriage, a cultivator, a sickle-bar mower, a hay tedder (for breaking up clumped green hay so it can dry), a dump rake (for raking cured hay into piles for pickup by hand), and a buckrake. A buckrake is used for gathering hay to build a haystack in the field. Philip Grant, a farmer born in 1926, says he would expect one to be paired with a beaverslide stacker, a machine that built very large haystacks (up to thirty feet high and weighing around twenty tons). Perhaps there used to be one in the Mannington area, but they are mostly wooden and too large to store indoors, so it would have rotted away. If there was one, one or more of the old-timers would likely remember it.

Five horse-drawn implements weren't very many, but many of their parts are wooden. This many decades after they were manufactured, any that are still sound have been under cover most of the time. We didn't go searching through farmers' barns.

Tractors and Implements

We didn't see as many tractors as I would have expected, but they must be there if people are no longer farming using only muscle power. What we saw were mostly John Deeres. All but one of them were quite small for the modern age, because most of the fields are too small for large equipment.

Looking at maps and aerial photographs doesn't convey the steepness of the land. Steep forestland is one thing, but you expect farmland to be flatter. The pastures and even hayfields are amazingly steep, right up to vertical and, in one case, overhanging ledge. Thinking pasture can be that steep, but not hay land, isn't accurate. Farmers need to clip pasture at least once a year or it grows up to species the animals won't graze. The steepness may be why horses continued to be used for so long and small tractors still dominate mechanical power so thoroughly. A small tractor has a lower center of gravity than a large one and so is less likely to roll over. A team of horses (or oxen) can handle even steeper land than a small tractor.

Of the tractors we saw, only the largest tractor we saw was certainly a diesel. The others could all be gasoline-powered, though small diesels are manufactured. As to age, the large one and one or two others could be post-2000, but the others are all older. Most are only moderately old, but the two at the Round Barn Museum are older still. There is a small steel-wheeled, hand-cranked Fordson from the twenties or early thirties. Philip Grant said the Fordsons used to be called man-killers because of their tendency to roll over backwards. There is also an Allis-Chalmers tractor from the late forties or early fifties. As an interesting aside, the same model was made during World War II but with steel wheels because of the rubber shortage. Most of them had their wheels cut down and rims welded on after the war so they could take rubber tires. The one in Grantville did not have that done, so we conclude it was built after the War.

There were also several skid-steer loaders. As with the implements, there were certainly some tractors that were out of sight when we were there, and we left a lot of road undriven. We saw quite a few implements, including five sickle-bar mowers, a rotary mower, four side-delivery hay rakes, four square hay balers (one of them very early), one round baler, and two hay tedders. There were wrapped bales, so there must be at least one bale wrapper, even though we didn't see it. (That innovation is recent enough I would not expect it to have been there in 2000. There wouldn't be a supply of plastic sheeting for it down-time anyway.) One of each of the following three-point hitch-mounted implements were present: two-bottom plow, rototiller, scraper, broadcast spreader for seeds and other light materials, and the remains of a post-hole digger. Finally, there was a loader-mounted bale spear for picking up round bales.

There were also uncounted numbers of stock trailers and other trailers, which may be pulled by either tractors or pickups. We saw plenty of pickups, but remarkably few trucks larger than a pickup. On the farms, there was just one that looked like a GMC from the mid-sixties. I have spotted others on farms in online aerial photography since then, but the resolution is poor.

And now for the pièce de résistance: a Wood Mizer. Wood Mizer is a brand of portable bandsaw sawmill powered by a mounted engine. When hitched behind a pickup or tractor, it can be moved to where the logs are, and saw them into lumber. It was incomplete, but that doesn't mean it was in 2000. In fact, its poor condition argues in favor of its having been present that long ago.

Not Seen

I cannot, of course, list them all, but here are a few that may be of interest: forage harvesters (aka corn choppers), corn pickers, combines, reaper-binders, mower conditioners, potato diggers, manure spreaders, harrows, farm bulldozers, cultipackers, Brillion seeders (which break up clods, sow small seed, and smooth and compact the soil in one pass), and heavier spreaders for materials such as lime. This does not mean there weren't any of those present in 2000. I would bet on the presence of at least one manure spreader and several harrows of one or more types. Probably one or more mower-conditioners, either cultipackers or Brillion seeders, and bulldozers. Definitely not combines or reaper-binders, likely not forage harvesters.

Implements Used Outside the Fields

Due to Covid-19, we were unable, in the two days we had there, to find someone who would let us into either the Round Barn Museum or the West Augusta Historical Society Museum. Nor did we ask to enter people's houses and outbuildings to see what they had.

However, we did see a few things by looking in the windows at the Round Barn Museum. There was a loom, a foot-pumped grindstone, and what looked like two corn shellers. There were several other things neither Jack nor I was able to identify, nor was Philip Grant upon being shown admittedly poor photographs (taken through windows).

We saw two cellar houses, which is to say, root cellars with small storage buildings above them. We also saw two tower silos, though one of them may have been just outside the Ring of Fire. That means the farms were once dairy farms. The Round Barn was also a dairy barn.

That is the limit of our evidence. Given the presence of so much horse-drawn equipment and what it says about the tendency of the locals to keep to the old ways, I would be very surprised if there were not quite a lot of smaller antique farm implements and tools in the area.

Conclusions

What does all this mean for the farms inside the Ring of Fire? The biggest change to our perceptions is that many—if not most—of the up-time farmers were already engaged in animal-powered agriculture. They would have a lot of equipment and know-how to pursue that. The shift to 1631 wouldn't change their lives all that much. They would be able to get in the harvest, in and after 1631, without taxing the supply of tractor power and its fuels. Also, bringing newly hired down-timers up to speed on the new implements would be far easier than with tractor power.

Copying the horse-drawn implements would be well within the capabilities of down-timer artisans. The implements would therefore be available sooner than if someone had to reinvent them. They would also be available sooner and in greater supply than if the up-timers had to build them with their limited machine shop facilities and trained personnel, which would initially be the case with most tractor-powered implements. They would also be available to more down-timer farmers than if the up-timers also needed to be supplied with them. However, many horse-drawn implements would have to wait for greater iron availability, though less so than the tractor-powered ones. As farming was a priority, some larger quantities of iron should be available to farm implement manufacturers ahead of general availability.

With such limited acreages of flat farmland, the up-timers would not have done extensive annual tillage. What there was would have been primarily home gardens. They were clearly heavily involved in pasturage and haymaking, and had the equipment to do it. That would support beef, dairy (cows or goats), sheep, horses, and several less common pastured species. They appear not to have had much equipment for other types of agriculture, so that will be a heavier lift for those trying to increase food production down-time.

* * *

In Memoriam

In Memoriam
Eric Flint
1947 - 2022

Eric Flint

Eric Flint studied African history; worked as a machinist; drove trucks; wrote, edited, and published books and short stories; and was a union organizer. He was married to Lucille Robbins and had a daughter, a son-in-law, and two grandchildren. He once posted a picture of himself wearing a shirt that said "Grumpa."

I think Eric liked to come across as grouchy. You could quickly see how much time he spent helping others out, though. That might be when he was risking his personal safety helping the unions or something as simple as taking a couple hours to make sure you understood where he wanted to go when he offered you a co-writing opportunity.

Eric's first novel was published when he was fifty years old. I count at least 69 novels as well as numerous anthologies, collections, novellas, and short stories. He wrote in several genres but was probably best known for alternate history. He didn't just write; he worked with others, especially helping new authors get started. Between the 1632 series and The Grantville Gazette, he helped over 200 authors be published. For about three-quarters of us, it was our first professional sale. That's aside from everything he did at Writers of the Future and the Superstars Writing Seminars.

As he often pointed out himself, the 1632 universe was less than half of Eric's writing. Of his many alternate history, science fiction, and fantasy universes, it's the one he opened to anyone who wanted to write in it. Sometimes he'd look bemused at the directions people took with it, but he'd let them do it, as long as it wasn't interfering with his own plans.

We are excited to help carry that legacy forward.

* * *

Jose J. Clavell

Jose Clavell

Jose Clavell served in the US Army, was a nurse at Walter Reed, and served in the Puerto Rico Wing of the Civil Air Patrol. He passed away in March, 2023.

In the 1632 universe, Jose developed the USE Marine Corps and the Naval Criminal Investigative Service. These are moving stories, and they're influential on other authors.

We'd like to keep Jose in the series.

FROM: CPT. L. KLINGL, USEN

TO: CDRE E. CANTRELL, USEN

—MESSAGE BEGINS—

RE: RETURN VOYAGE

FOLLOWING OPERATION "ISLAND HOPPERS" AND HURRICANE, CAPTURED

PIRATE SHIPS LOW ON FRESH WATER. TWO VESSELS DIVERTED TO PUERTO RICO AND HOVE TO OFF LOCATION LABELED MAYAGUEZ ON UP-

TIME MAP. REFILLED WATER. NO ENEMY CONTACT. STOP

COMMEND USEMC SGT. J. CLAVELL FOR INITIATIVE LOCATING FRESH WATER AND ESTABLISHING CACHES AND DEFENSIVE POSITIONS FOR FUTURE OPERATIONS. STOP

HOWEVER SGT. CLAVELL LEFT USE FLAG. CLAIMS WE OWN ISLAND. STOP

—MESSAGE ENDS—

"I dunno, Clavell." Hans Ludolf squinted. His nose was scrunched up, and his lips pursed, all signs that the Marine was very skeptical about something. "I think the captain is pissed."

"Hard to tell, from how he was trying not to laugh the whole time," Clavell countered.

"What if the Spanish find that flag? They will search the area. They might find the caches and fighting positions."

"Then they will think there are patrols on the island and waste a lot of time and many more resources than we left in the caches," Clavell returned. "And if one of our ships passes between Puerto Rico and Hispaniola and needs food and water . . . It is what the up-timers call a win-win. And who knows? We could find ourselves back there someday."

* * *

Key Storyline Points

This section is both orientation and review for readers and writers. It necessarily contains spoilers. If you don't like spoilers, we recommend skipping to the next article or downloading a copy of *1632* from the Baen Free Library: https://www.baen.com/1632.html

Timeline

Sunday, April 2, 2000 - Rita Stearns and Tom Simpson are married in her hometown Grantville, WV. Rita's brother Mike Stearns was president of the United Mine Workers of America local, so many coal miners and their families were at the reception in the high school cafeteria. Tom Simpson was the starting nose guard for the WVU Mountaineers. His parents came down from Pittsburgh, although they did not approve of the marriage.

Sunday, May 25, 1631 - An Assiti shard moved a sphere a little over six miles in diameter to Thuringia, in the Germanies, during the Thirty Years War. It appeared just a few days after the sack of Magdeburg, arguably the single greatest atrocity of the war. Mike, Police Chief Dan Frost, and several miners break up an atrocity just over the border of the Ring of Fire and rescue Balthasar and Rebecca Abrabanel.

Wednesday, May 28, 1631 - A town meeting is held in the high school gym. After Mike's "I say we start the American Revolution one hundred and fifty years early" speech, he is elected chairman of the Emergency Committee.

Monday, June 30, 1631 - Up-timers and Alexander Mackay's Scots defeat a *tercio* and liberate Badenburg in the Battle of the Crapper. Jeff Higgins rescues Gretchen Richter.

Wednesday, September 17, 1631 - King Gustav II Adolf's Swedish army defeats Count Tilly's Imperial Army at Breitenfeld. In the new timeline, this battle plays out very much the same as it did in our timeline.

Early October, 1631 - A fragment of Tilly's scattered forces marches on Jena. Grantville sends a mix of up-time and down-time forces. The battle is fought almost entirely by sniper Julie Simms.

December, 1631 - Mike Stearns is elected President of the New United States.

August, 1632 - Cardinal Richelieu engineers a multi-pronged attack on Grantville. Imperial mercenary commander Albrecht von Wallenstein designates the high school as the main target. NUS forces are victorious at Eisenach, the Wartburg, Suhl, and downtown Grantville. Captain Gars arrives with Swedish, Finnish, and Lapp troops, and the combined forces defeat the Croats at Grantville High School.

September, 1632 - NUS and Swedish forces shatter Wallenstein's army in the Battle of Alte Veste outside Nuremberg. In contrast to our timeline, Gustav II Adolf does not need to retreat from Nuremberg, and there is no battle of Lützen for him to die in.

Fall, 1631 - Gustav II Adolf and Mike Stearns organized the Confederated Principalities of Europe.

Characters

The city of Grantville is the collective protagonist of the 1632 series. Eric pointed to these eight as his main characters. If more than one of these couples is present, you're reading a "main line" book.

Rebecca Abrabanel - young Jewish woman born in England and raised in Amsterdam

Jeff Higgins - high school senior, D&D aficionado

Alexander Mackay - captain of a company of Scots cavalry in the Swedish army

Melissa Mailey - high school English teacher

James Nichols - African-American doctor from Chicago, in town because his daughter Sharon was one of Rita's bridesmaids

Gretchen Richter - young German woman taken captive by mercenaries

Julie Simms - captain of the cheerleading team, potential biathlon competitor

Michael Stearns - coal miner and UMWA union local president

Terms, Concepts, and Groups of People

Committees of Correspondence - organized to spread up-time ideals, leaders include Gretchen Richter, Gunter Achterhof, and Joachim von Thierbach ("Spartacus")

Down-timer - a person born in the sixteenth or seventeenth century

Up-timer - one of the approximately 3,551 West Virginians who came through the Ring of Fire

* * *

Coming Tuesday, September 5, 2023

1638: The Sovereign States

Eric Flint, Paula Goodlett, Gorg Huff

The United Sovereign States of Russia struggles to set in place the traditions and legal precedents that will let it turn into a constitutional monarchy with freedom and opportunity for all its citizens.

At the same time, they're trying to balance the power of the states and the federal government. And the USSR is fighting a civil war with Muscovite Russia, defending the new state of Kazakh from invasion by the Zunghars, building a tech base and an economy that will allow its money to be accepted in western Europe, establishing a more solid claim to Siberia, and, in general, keeping the wheels of civilization from coming off and dumping Russia back into the Time of Troubles. Or, possibly even worse, reinstalling the sort of repressive oligarchy that they just got rid of.

* * *

Connect with
Eric Flint's 1632 & Beyond

Eric Flint's 1632 & Beyond would love to hear from you! You can connect with us through:

Email: 1632andBeyond@1632andBeyond.com

Shop: 1632Magazine.com

Author Site: Author.1632Magazine.com

Facebook: Facebook.com/t1632andBeyond

Pinterest: 1632andBeyond

Instagram: 1632andBeyond

Because reviews really do matter, especially for small publishers and indie authors, please take a few minutes to post a review on Amazon, Goodreads, or wherever you find books, and don't forget to tell your friends to check us out!

You are welcome to join us on **BaensBar.net**. Most of t
he chatting about 1632 on the Bar is in the 1632 Tech forum. If you want to read and comment on possible future stories, check out 1632 Slush (stories) and 1632 Slush Comments on BaensBar.net.

If you are interested in writing in the 1632 universe, that's fabulous! For more information, visit **Author.1632Magazine.com**

Made in the USA
Middletown, DE
27 September 2023

39261945R00086